THE PRISONER OF GUN HILL

When Luke Walsh falls for the beautiful Dee Dee Bright, he makes the biggest mistake of his young life. After she tricks him into killing the marshal of Tucson, Arizona, there is nothing for it but to take to the desert. But when his horse founders, he finds himself afoot and alone on the plain. Picked up by a passing wagon, he is set to work as slave labour in the Gun Hill gold mine — the remote outpost harbouring a nest of dangerous outlaws . . .

OWEN G. IRONS

THE PRISONER OF GUN HILL

Complete and Unabridged

LINFORD
Leicester

First published in Great Britain in 2013 by
Robert Hale Limited
London

First Linford Edition
published 2015
by arrangement with
Robert Hale Limited
London

A catalogue record for this book is available
from the British Library.

ISBN 978–1–4448–2358–5

Published by
F. A. Thorpe (Publishing)
Anstey, Leicestershire

Set by Words & Graphics Ltd.
Anstey, Leicestershire
Printed and bound in Great Britain by
T. J. International Ltd., Padstow, Cornwall

This book is printed on acid-free paper

1

He didn't like being a killer.

Luke Walsh felt that he was already being tormented adequately by a bad decision. He needed no hell like the one he was passing through. The purgatory wind of the white desert buffeted him as he rode on across interminable miles of sand. The wind bent back the brim of his Stetson and threatened to blow it from his head. He could not lose his hat — not out here. He paused to drop the drawstring and run the bead up along the two strands, tightening it under his chin. As he did so he lifted his eyes to the ranks of serrated, chocolate-colored hills ahead of him. He reached for his canteen and was able to milk a drop or two from it.

His big gray horse was shuddering under him, lathered with foam, nearly ridden to death. There was nothing

Luke could do for the animal. He had no water, he could not pause to rest. They were back there, somewhere, following. The hot desert breeze continued to blow fitfully. It tugged at his clothing with hot grasping fingers. Luke had not seen a signpost, but he was certain that he had made a wrong turn and ridden directly into Hades.

He rode on, the horse foundering beneath him. Luke's body collected no perspiration; the wind evaporated it before it could collect, denying him even that much cooling. His tongue had begun to cleave to his palate and his lower lip was split open. The sun was raising blisters on the back of his neck despite his hat now being tugged as low as it would ride.

The sand began to grow thinner, whisked away by the gusting wind, and he found himself looking across a vast playa, the remains of an ancient sea. It stretched out bleakly toward the distant hills where he hoped to find water even though he was not familiar with them.

He and his gray horse were the only living creatures on the vast expanse. Not a rattlesnake, perching bird or crawling insect could survive on the playa. All creatures require some sort of moisture to survive.

Luke squinted against the glare of the sun, reflected now off the patchwork of dried clay molded by the passing eons into cracked, haphazardly shaped tiles. His horse shuddered again and made a pitiable sound in its throat. This was it, then. He glanced behind him at the white-sand desert and considered going back. It was a brief, desperate thought. There was nothing back there. He would only be giving the land a second chance at killing him, and riding back toward his pursuers, and there surely must be men pursuing him, men on fresher horses, better outfitted and supplied with water for the trek.

He took one moment to damn that faithless Dee Dee Carson and started his faltering gray out on to the endless stretch of gray-white playa.

The sun was now lowering itself behind him as he continued his eastward ride. But the demon sky was not cooling; it seemed to grow hotter, and the wind that he had cursed abated and left the desert flats a breathless frying pan. Luke felt his horse stumble again and he tried to jerk its head up, but it would not rise and the gray plodded on, the hard-baked playa under its hoofs too dry to even raise dust as they passed. Something odd, bright red and angry flickered across the desert wasteland, drew closer and struck Luke in the eyes.

When he opened his eyes, he found himself flat on his back against the heated clay of the playa. Confused, he tried to sit up, found that he could not. He couldn't understand how this had happened until he realized that he was lying next to his faithful gray, that the animal was dead and already stiffening. From somewhere a group of all-knowing buzzards had appeared over them. A dozen, two dozen. Soon there would be hundreds of the carrion birds. They, too, had to have moisture to survive, and theirs was extracted from flesh.

It took long minutes for Luke to drag himself backwards on his palms and sit up, resting his back against the dead horse, the silver-white sun in his eyes.

Well, then, he thought. This was the end, unless he moved, got to his feet and somehow found crude shelter. He would have to do that or die where he sat. On his knees he pulled his Winchester rifle from its boot, unstrapped his saddle-bags from the saddle ties and with one massive surge of his flagging strength, managed to pull the bags from underneath the downed horse. Exhausted with the effort, he slung the saddle-bags over his shoulder and sat down again, unsure if he could continue onward.

Probably because the whipping devil wind had died down, perspiration now began to trickle into his eyes, down his throat and under his arms. It did nothing to cool him. It seemed now to Luke that he had two choices: to die where he sat, or to stagger ahead as far as he could and die there. Only one of these options held even the smallest bit of hope.

He turned and rose, using the horse's body to lever himself to his feet.

He walked on.

If, in fact, his stumbling, staggering gait could be called walking. He veered left and right like a drunk. Finally, inevitably, he fell. He skidded face first against the hot, unyielding surface of the playa, which was as solid as ceramic tile; he remained there, his arms outflung, his hat lost beneath his body. He would rise again. Soon, he promised himself, but his first attempt to do so was a failure as was his second an hour or so later. His movements were uncoordinated, his limbs unresponsive. It was as if all of his body had given up the will to live. Except for his mind, which urged him to do something, try *anything* to survive.

But there was nothing to do but die. He closed his eyes against the glare of the sun and waited to find out what it was like to be dead.

Something jerked at him. Something rolled him over and raised him to a seated position. He was roughly handled, and then thrown on to his back again. This place was just as hard as the desert earth, but somehow different. Luke's head felt wet, as if someone had dumped a bucket of water over it, which was exactly what had been done. He opened one swollen eye to discover that he was lying in the back of a heavy wagon carrying lumber. Used lumber, judging by its weather-grayed, splintered appearance.

Someone, then, had found him and was taking him . . . somewhere.

Or maybe he was dead and this was the burial party. He shook the absurd notion out of his mind and tried to lift his head to see who was driving the large wagon, where they might be headed, but it required too much effort and he lay back again, listening to the metronomic beating of the mules' hoofs as they traversed the wide desert, going . . . somewhere. Which was a better place than the nowhere he had imagined ending up.

He found he could not sleep, but in the end it didn't matter. The bright red thing appeared again and he simply passed out in the bed of the freight wagon as it wended its way toward its uncertain destination.

Only half-alert, he heard someone say, 'No sense in letting him die now.' Someone clambered from the seat of the freight wagon into its bed and again poured water over his head. Some of it streamed toward his moisture-starved mouth. Luke sucked in the remarkably delicious, life-saving trickle of refreshment.

He thought he nodded his thanks, but it might have been more a thought than reality.

The wagon rolled on; it was moving noticeably slower now, apparently climbing a grade. Luke, still only half-aware of what was happening to him, thought he could smell the pungent scent of mountain juniper. Had they made it into the foothills then? So soon?

He realized he had no idea of how long they had been traveling, so it might have been possible. He had faded in and out of consciousness the day long as the punishing desert sun crept across the sky. A shadow crossed his face and he opened his eyes. The shadow had been cast by a single cedar tree standing beside the trail. So they were in the hills, on the flanks of the chocolate mountains. The temperature seemed not to have fallen; his ride had gotten no more comfortable; his future looked no brighter, except that he now had a future of some sort.

He must have been a pathetic figure if anyone were looking at him, which no one was: sunburnt, blistered by the heat, hair lank, clothes torn, eyes nearly sealed shut, his body battered in the fall from his horse.

But he was alive.

No thanks to Dee Dee Bright. That was not the name she had been christened with, but it was what she called herself. Not many women in her profession used their real names. He had met her in Tucson, Arizona while traveling with the Havasu Ranch bunch, and decided that it might be a good idea to stop over awhile. Dee Dee had that effect on men.

She was an entertainer, a hostess at one of the larger saloons in Tucson, the Hamilton House. Well, those were the words she used to describe her profession. In truth she was one of the many women who have discovered that taking off her clothing for lonely men is an easy way to avoid doing work of any sort. It paid well and seldom got her hurt. It beat washing pots and pans in some hot kitchen.

Luke wasn't trying to rescue her; she had gotten beyond that point, but he was willing to help her when she explained her predicament.

'Virgil Sly is back in town. I saw him.

He sent a note to me saying he wants to take me with him,' Dee Dee said as they sat on the edge of her bed with its flouncy blue coverlet. Luke nodded. He had been in Arizona Territory long enough to have heard of Virgil Sly. A killer with a fast gun and an ugly attitude. Half of the law enforcement agencies in Arizona were looking for him. He was shadowy, slippery, and he had once been Dee Dee's lover before he had been forced to flee Tucson after holding up the Union Bank, killing a teller and a stander-by.

'I know you won't believe this,' Dee Dee said softly, 'but he is the only man I ever could love. The rest are just bookmarks in my life. Virgil thinks we can make it to Mexico without getting caught. He says he's enough money for us to live there comfortably the rest of our lives.'

Which he probably did, considering the numbers of robberies he was reputed to have staged.

'I hope it works out for you, then,'

Luke said, feeling a little uneasy. Her small, pale hands gripped his work-hardened sun-browned one.

'We haven't known each other long, Luke, but you've treated me right and I count you as a friend.' Moist blue eyes lifted to his. 'I need you to help us.'

'Me?' Luke asked, stunned. He didn't know the law, but did know that any help he gave a criminal like Virgil Sly was illegal.

'I can see you don't understand what I'm trying to tell you,' Dee Dee said, letting her hands fall away. She rose and walked to the window of her room, the sunlight streaming prettily through the sheer fabric of her negligee. 'I'm in danger, Luke,' she told him, suddenly swirling to face him, her eyes still damp.

'Tell me about it,' Luke encouraged, still dubious.

'A man who used to ride with Virgil, a man named Cotton Werth, is looking for Virgil — that's the reason Virgil hasn't been to meet me. Cotton thinks that Virgil cheated him out of the proceeds from certain . . . endeavors.'

'No honesty among thieves?' Luke suggested.

'I've heard that before, but Virgil isn't like that.' She sat on the bed again and sighed. 'But Cotton Werth is convinced that it is so.' She waved a hand in the air. 'Oh, it's all too complicated to be explained.' She settled for: 'Cotton Werth thinks he was shorted and he's mad. So mad that he's been to the town marshal's office and told Marshal Stoddard that Virgil is in town.'

Luke frowned. Even among criminals, that was out of bounds. You don't rat on your friends to the law.

'And so?' Luke prodded.

'And so Virgil cannot come to meet me. Marshal Will Stoddard has men watching all around the Hamilton. Virgil can't get to me and I can't sneak out to meet him.'

'I see,' Luke replied, 'and just what is it you're planning to do, and what do you want me to do?'

'Nothing illegal,' she told him, taking

his hand once again, sincerity filling her pale blue eyes. She gulped twice, then turned her eyes down and told him, 'I told you Virgil has been sending me notes. If we can't manage to shake Cotton Werth, we'll never get to Mexico. Virgil has asked me to invite Werth up to my room a little after midnight.

'Virgil wants to offer Werth a share of the money that Werth claims is due him in exchange for our freedom. Werth can always tell Marshal Stoddard that he had news that Virgil had escaped from town and was headed for Flagstaff, or somewhere. Any story will do. Then the marshal will lift his surveillance, you see.'

'Do you think Werth will go for it?'

'Why wouldn't he? This all started over money; it's all he cares about.'

That made a kind of sense. Luke ran his eyes over Dee Dee, from her sleek dark hair to her small, somehow beautiful feet. He was grateful to her for having let him know her. He knew it was never going to be a lasting arrangement — she was not that sort of woman. She had a man she loved. The killer, Virgil Sly. He didn't like it, but the words spilled out of his mouth.

'What do you want me to do?' he asked again.

'Just this,' Dee Dee said, bouncing excitedly on the bed as if she were a young girl. 'Cotton Werth can be dangerous — he's one of those Red Butte boys, and they're all wild. Virgil can't be around to protect me, so I would like you to just be near by in case Werth doesn't like the offer, or in case he tries to . . . ' her voice trailed off, and Luke thought he knew what she meant.

He considered the plan for a long minute, took a deep breath and said, 'If that's all you want — someone to make sure Werth doesn't hurt you, I can do that.'

'You're a generous man, Luke Walsh,' Dee Dee said, pulling him down to her on the bed. She was generous as well.

15

After midnight, as Luke stood in the shadows of the Hamilton House's alley, he shivered slightly in the chill of the night. He was clothed only in jeans and a light flannel shirt. Hunching his shoulders, hands thrust deep in his pockets, he pondered the wisdom of the bargain he had made with Dee Dee Bright.

He did not know Werth, did not know his inclinations. He had only the vaguest of descriptions of the man. Yet despite Virgil Sly's well-known perfidiousness, he was Dee Dee's man and she deserved a chance at a little happiness after the life she had led. Or so he had convinced himself. Even if all went well, if Werth could be bought off and they could elude Marshal Will Stoddard, they would have to live life on the run, even if they made it to Mexico. That, he knew, was none of his business and there was no point in telling that to Dee Dee.

She only wanted to be with her man, and even if it included a rough ride across the desert with men pursuing them, she would have her moment. Luke Walsh had promised her that, reckless promise though it might have been.

As he stood shivering in the darkness a lantern flickered on behind Dee Dee's upstairs window. He thought he heard low voices communicating. He moved slowly toward the outside door of the Hamilton and slipped inside. No one was watching. Strangers came and went at all hours of the night. Luke stood looking up the stairwell by the narrow light of a lantern.

Dee Dee screamed.

'Help me. Someone please help me!' Luke was bounding up the stairs, pistol drawn. Something had gone wrong. It seemed that Dee Dee's mistrust of Werth was well-founded. Rushing toward her room, Luke slammed his shoulder against the wood of the door; it opened with a splintering of wood around the latch. Dee Dee was flat on her back on her blue bed. On top of her was a bulky man without clothing. All Luke could see was rounded white flesh and a curious look of surprise as the man's head turned toward him.

Luke fired twice, the Colt bucking in his hand, filling the room with acrid gunsmoke. The sound of the shots was still echoing in his ears as the fat man rolled off Dee Dee and slammed against the floor, dead.

'That worked out all right, then!' Dee Dee said, sitting up in bed, nude to the waist. There was a satisfied smile on her full lips. Luke started to cross the room, saw the strange man's clothing folded neatly on the wooden chair, his coat positioned over its back. There was a shiny badge pinned to it.

Luke didn't have to ask. He already knew that he had just killed Marshal Will Stoddard.

2

Luke figured he would never know if the plan Virgil Sly and his girlfriend had devised had worked out. He only knew that he had been suckered into killing the Tucson marshal by a bit of leg and a false smile. A man never seems to learn. Dee Dee had obviously invited Stoddard up to her midnight room for the sole purpose of having him killed. When Luke, pushing in like some false cavalier, had made his play, he had ended every chance he had ever had for his own advancement in life.

He had become a vagrant killer in the long desert, presumably pursued by a posse, his life dependent on his horse, which was not strong enough in the end to preserve it.

Now he was . . . where was he? What was he? Who were these men he found himself traveling with — if lying inert on the bed of a freight wagon can be called traveling with someone. There was a burlap sack filled with potatoes stuffed under his head as a pillow. Other similar sacks holding some sort of supplies were strewn around him. He opened an eye; even that smallest of movements seemed painful. He caught a glimpse of a yellow half moon, of scraggly, water-deprived juniper and desert cedar trees. He knew they were ascending a trail by the tug of gravity on his battered body. Now and then the wagon hit a chuck hole or a stretch of washboard, which might have been what jolted him alert in the first place. If his present state of awareness could be called being alert.

More trees appeared, dusty and stunted, and the moon cast shadows through them. It was cooler now; the dying sun had tucked itself away beyond the horizon, heading toward the distant sea. They had gained altitude. Enough to cool the searing heat of day. The trees, wretched unkempt creatures that they were, seemed to aid the coolness.

Luke did not feel strong enough yet to try lifting himself to look around. It was another hour on, perhaps two, when the land seemed to level and the wagon turned in an arc and ground to a halt as the driver reined in the horses. Artificial light flared up from somewhere and a man approached the wagon, carrying a lantern.

This individual with a face like a grizzly bear held the lantern over the wagon bed and grunted with satisfaction.

'The lumber will do, Frank. And I see you brought us a man as well. Good!'

The rest of the conversation was lost to Luke as the man with the lantern moved to the front of the wagon. No matter, Luke Walsh was again absent from the world, passed out, no more aware than a dead man.

★　★　★

'He doesn't look like much to me,' the woman was saying.

'He'll do. He's young. All he needs is water and food and a few days rest. We can use him.'

Through the slits of his eyelids, Luke looked up, seeing that the woman hovering over his bed was gray, stout and stern-appearing. The man — Frank? — from the wagon told her, 'He'll do. Just give him water now and then and spoon him up some of that leftover stew.'

'I wasn't brought up to be a nurse,' she snapped back at him.

'Then have Susan do it. We want him to get well, don't we?'

By the dim uncertain light of the lantern on the wall, Luke saw them turn and exit the room. She wide and determined, he bent and uncertain. The heavy plank door was banged shut again and Luke closed his eyes once more, eager for sleep although he was not tired. He was battered, sun-burnt, thirsty and hungry. Sleep would solve none of that, but it was a place to descend to where none of that would matter so much.

Again he lost track of time. There had been the moon shining in the window when they carried him into the small room and plopped him down on the rough, narrow bed. Now when he looked toward the window he could not see the faintest glow of moonlight. The lantern continued to burn although the wick was smoking and fizzling as if it were running out of fuel.

The blonde girl slipped into the room, carrying a water pitcher. She placed this down on a bedside table, walked to the lantern, adjusted the wick and returned to frown down at Luke Walsh.

'Got yourself into a fix, didn't you?' the young woman asked. 'Are you wanting some water?'

'Please, yes.'

Silently then she handed Luke a mug half-filled with water. He knew that she was trying to prevent him from drinking too much at once. He drank what there was in three long swallows, feeling the coolness of it swim through his body. Remarkable stuff to the deprived: water. Sweet, cool, nourishing, saving. Magical elixir, that.

After draining the mug he let his head fall back on to the thick pillow.

'I've heated up some leftover beef stew for you,' the blonde girl said. 'You may not feel like eating much of it, but even a few spoonfuls will help you.' She bent low and squinted at his face. Luke was aware of the scent of lye soap on her, and the distant hint of lilac. 'I'll bring some butter in. It will help your cracked lips.'

'Thank you . . . Susan, isn't it?' She rocked back, surprised.

'How did you know that?'

'I heard your name mentioned. Frank and the older woman were discussing you.'

'Oh,' she said, studying him quizzically for a moment. 'I'll be back in a few minutes. I'm going to fetch you a bowl of stew.' She turned toward the door, paused and turned around. 'You'll be all right in a few days, from what I can see. That's when your real trouble will begin.'

Before Luke could ask a question she scurried from the room, the hem of her blue-checked gingham dress making whispering sounds across the floor. He lay in bed wondering what Susan had meant by that parting remark. No matter. For now he was alive, being tended, fed and rested. Whatever was to come would just have to be endured as a sort of penance for the killing of Marshal Stoddard and repayment for having his life saved from the burning jaws of the desert.

Luke ate twice that evening and drank more water, had butter applied to his split lips and slept again, more satisfactorily. Morning was a haze of golden light through the high window of his room. Through this he could see the gently stirring tips of the trees standing near the house. He felt renewed but not strong. His joints ached. He thought that if he had to he would be able to get to his feet and hobble away, but there was no need to try moving just yet. Where would he go?

Susan returned to his room some hours later, looking fresh. Smelling sweet. She still wore the blue gingham dress, but she had pinned her hair up in some fashion known only to women. She looked away almost shyly as she delivered a tray with hot-cakes and bacon on it. She placed a cup of coffee on the night table. It steamed pleasantly into the morning air.

'I wish I thought I could eat all of this,' Luke said, taking the tray with gratitude.

'Do what you can with it,' Susan answered, still not letting her eyes meet his.

'Tomorrow,' Luke said while cutting himself a wedge of hotcakes, 'I'll be up and about.' He tried to smile, but it hurt his lips. She turned her back to

him, shrugged her narrow shoulders
and left the room. Well, then, she was in
no mood for conversation on this
morning, Luke decided. Still, as he ate
he considered that something was not
right around this house. What, he could
not guess and did not try to as he
finished as many of the hotcakes as he
could, drank most of the coffee and lay
down to sleep once again.

Boston was tugging at his toes, trying
to wake him up. He knew the man with
the grizzly-bear head was named
Boston because that was what Frank
called him as he said, 'No sense to be
rough with him, Boston.'

'Rough? That ain't rough,' Boston
said. 'If you think that it is, you've never
seen rough.'

'I only meant . . . ' the slender, bent
man named Frank started to say.

'Look, he's eaten our food, been
laying up in bed under your roof for
two days. Wasn't for us he'd be dead
now — you know that's true. It's time
for him to get up and get to work

repaying us. It's time we started him on the shaft.'

'I doubt he's up to it yet,' Frank appealed. His wrinkled, long-chinned face was sagging with the concerns of age.

'He'll be all right. He's still a pup, Frank. We'll get him started today at least. If it proves too much, I'll let him knock off early. But we've got to get to work, Frank. You know that.'

'I suppose so,' Frank said.

'Billy can't handle the timbers on his own.'

'No,' Frank said, defeated. The old, hunched man came nearer Luke's bed. 'You got to rise and shine, brother. The piper's calling the tune.'

Shaking his head, clearing the sleep-dust from his eyes, Luke Walsh swung his feet to the floor, understanding none of the other men's conversation except that they wanted him to get up. It was their house; he had no choice but to comply. Besides, he was tired of being on his back. He looked past the two men in the pre-dawn gray of his room hoping, irrationally, to see Susan. Of course she was not there.

He was no longer considered a patient.

'Toss me my jeans and my boots, boys, and I'll join you as soon as I can,' he said.

Dressing himself was easier said than done. Standing and putting his legs into his jeans took more time than he had expected. Tugging on his well-worn boots was about as easy as pushing a freight train. Face it — he was still beat up, heat-cramped, bruised, fluid-deprived and groggy. With his boots and jeans in place, he had to sit on the edge of the bed, breathing roughly. Had he aged fifty years overnight?

Beyond the window the cobalt sky showed. The moon had settled into its daytime sleeping place; there was the faint rosy glow of dawn. Luke did not want to get up and finish out the day, but after all, he reflected, he did owe these men for saving his life, for taking him in and feeding him. He would do what he could for them, even though his condition was not good and it was not clear what they required. Any given favors deserve repayment — especially when it was one's life that had been given.

He rose heavily and found his yellow flannel shirt on a chair. It had still not been washed and had the stink of man-smell, his own, about it. He smiled — what had he expected? For them to do his laundry for him? Fastening the snaps, he tucked the shirttails in. He looked for his hat, found it on a bureau and searched around for his guns.

No luck there. His Colt and the Winchester were missing from the room.

He supposed that was not important at the time. He would ask about them later. The men who had taken such care to ensure his survival were unlikely to abruptly kill him — or so he believed. Luke was staggering a little, his familiar high-heeled boots seeming uncomfortable. He tugged the plank door open wide and went out into a corridor which led two ways. He could smell breakfast cooking to his right, so he automatically turned that way. The passage led him into the kitchen where Susan, aproned now, was frying half a dozen eggs in a large black iron skillet while coffee boiled on the stove plate.

'They asked me to get up,' he said to her back. Still feeling wobbly, he leaned against the door jamb for support. For a moment he thought she was not going to turn around or even answer. She glanced at him after turning the eggs and offered him a wan smile.

'They would. The breakfast table is through that door.'

That seemed to be the end of the conversation, so Luke made his unsteady way through the door and into a low-ceilinged room where Boston, Frank and a blond kid with nervous eyes sat around the table sipping coffee.

'Glad you could join us,' Frank said as Luke lowered himself heavily into the chair opposite the old man.

'I just barely made it,' Luke replied.

'I can see that,' Frank answered. Then to the bulky man beside him, 'Boston, I can't see how this man can be of any help today. He's just about knackered.'

'He'll be all right,' Boston said, leaning back and stroking his silver-gray beard. 'I'm sure he wants to keep up his end of things around here.' He let his chair slap forward and put his forearms on the table. 'Isn't that right?' His bearish black eyes were menacing.

'I'll do what I can,' Luke agreed in a neutral tone.

Susan entered the room carrying a tray with the eggs and bacon. The men wasted no time in digging in. Luke couldn't blame them — there isn't much to be said for cold fried eggs.

'I didn't know you were coming for breakfast,' Susan told him. 'I'll have your food in a few minutes.'

'Thank you,' Luke said, feeling like the outsider he was as he sat with an empty plate on the table before him while the others ate with muffled grunts and sounds of enjoyment. His own meal was delivered as Boston lifted his grizzly head from his work, dabbed at his beard with a napkin and directed his gaze to Luke Walsh.

'I'm Boston Sears. Have you heard of me?'

'No,' Luke said. 'I'm not from around here.'

'No one's from around here. Only a fool would settle in these lonesome mountains. But that doesn't matter. This here's Frank Rafferty, if you didn't know. And the kid there is Billy Rafferty.'

'Susan's brother?' Luke asked. The blond kid smiled. 'People always ask that. Actually she's my second cousin. I got dropped on Uncle Frank here.'

'Indians,' Frank Rafferty managed to grumble. There had to be a long story behind the kid's ending up on this forsaken hill with his distant uncle, but now wasn't the time to ask about it.

'Probably wondering why I had

Frank bring you here,' Boston said as Luke continued to work at his breakfast. 'It wasn't human kindness — we need men to work up here. Do you have any idea how hard it is to get supplies of any kind up here? I mean anything a man needs — or a woman,' he said, glancing toward the kitchen door where Susan had reappeared, standing with her arms crossed, tilted against the door frame. A strand of blond hair had drifted free of its pins to fall across her face.

'I can imagine,' Luke said, answering Boston's probably rhetorical question.

'You'd have to cross the desert to find materials and then recross it to drag them up the hill. Forks, spoons, blankets, anything you can name,' Boston said in his deep voice that seemed blended with gravel. 'Now consider how hard it is to find a man willing to come out here to work.'

'For money, men have been known to endure a lot,' Luke replied. 'Isolation, deprivation . . .'

'Those we have,' Boston said. 'What we don't have is money.'

Luke nodded his understanding and pushed his plate away, returning to his cup of now-cold coffee. 'That would make matters difficult.'

'Frank and Billy made a two-day trek to Tucson hoping to find some used lumber. When they came across you, there was only two things they could have done — let you die or enlist you to help us in our endeavors. To work for us without pay.'

'I understand that, I honestly do,' Luke answered. 'I've already said that I'll do what I can to repay my debt. My life, such as it is, means something to me.'

'We understand each other, then,' Boston Sears said, but there was no smile on his lips.

'I think so,' Luke replied. 'I needed some help; you need some help up here. It's a fair trade.' He paused, placed his coffee cup down and said, 'I was wondering where my pistol and my rifle have gotten to. I've grown kind of attached to them.'

'They're put away,' Frank Rafferty, who had said nothing during the discussion, answered.

'Can't see why you'd have any use for them up here,' Boston said. His eyes were smug and cold. 'And since you're going to be staying around for a while, having weapons in your possession doesn't matter, does it?'

'I suppose not,' Luke said, 'it's just that a Western man hates to go around feeling naked — I'm sure you understand,' he added, noticing that Boston's own gunbelt was slung around his hips.

'We're all friends here,' Boston said severely, 'at least we should be.'

Billy Rafferty started to pipe in, chirping a word or two, but fell silent again as Boston's eyes switched to him. The sun had grown bright beyond the windows, illuminating the stark landscape beyond.

'It's time you got some work done,' Boston said to Billy. Luke was included in the order, he knew. The two men rose from the breakfast table and went out as Frank and Boston engaged in some sort of private conversation. Billy walked to the shanty tool shed as Luke looked out over the land. The chocolate-colored hills, now red at their tips as the sun rose behind them, folded and jumbled together in patternless ways. Canyons fell away into the still night-shadowed clefts. There was much nopal and cholla cactus growing on their flanks. On the higher ground stood clumps of stunted juniper and an occasional wind-twisted cedar tree.

The land on the slopes jutted out in oddly angled layers, sometimes appearing like precise steps, at others they jutted upward, pressed into slanting tiers by the ancient forces of nature. It was a desolate, somehow disturbing sight. By noon, when the sun had crested the high ridges, Luke guessed that it would be desert-hot again on this side of the hills.

Billy Rafferty had returned from the

tool shed with two pickaxes and two round-pointed shovels over his shoulders. He handed the shovels to Luke and carried the heavier picks himself.

'What's the plan?' Luke asked, falling in beside Billy as the blond youth trudged up the rock-strewn hillside toward higher ground.

'We dig,' Billy said. He paused and looked at Luke Walsh in puzzlement. 'Didn't anybody tell you anything?'

'No. I've been asleep most of the time since I've been here. What are we digging?'

'A mine shaft,' Billy said, starting on his way up the path again. Luke lifted his eyes to the rising face of dark bluff before them.

'In that?' he asked, studying the daunting land-form.

'In that,' Billy answered. 'Since it's been done before, Boston and my Uncle Frank are convinced it can be done again. I don't know — I've been at it six months now and haven't hardly made a dent.'

'Digging — pick and shovel work — in this heat?' Luke said in astonishment. Billy must have had more muscle than showed through his thin shirt. Billy Rafferty shrugged.

'Uncle Frank told me to do it, and I have no choice, do I? He and Susan are my only family. The rest of them were killed in an attack by White Mountain Apaches. I've got to earn my keep.'

'I guess the same goes for me,' Luke replied. 'Though I won't be of much help just yet.'

'Any little help is appreciated,' Billy said, puffing. They had managed to struggle up the rugged path until they reached a shelf of land which appeared to have been man-made. To Luke's right was the dark entrance to a cavern, also man-made.

'Is that it?' he asked Billy.

Billy's eyes flickered that way, and he answered, 'No! That's the old mine. The one that was worth digging for Gunn, but didn't prove out for us. This is our recent work,' he said, indicating a shallow concave indentation in the red rock bluff before them. If Billy had been at that for six months, the stone was definitely solid. Under his breath Luke muttered a wondering curse.

He hated to plead, but he was still in pretty bad shape, his body battered. He asked, 'How are the chances of me sitting down for a minute or two before we start work?'

'Sure,' Billy said with a grin. 'I always do. They can't see us from the cabin.'

They planted themselves on two nearby boulders still in shadow from the looming bluff, and Luke looked out over the raw land again. Now he could see the flat playa and the encroachment of the white sand dunes beyond that. It was a wonder that he had crossed that and was still alive.

'Don't your uncle and Boston ever help you dig?' he asked Billy.

'Nah. Well, you've seen how Frank moves. His back is all hunched over with something like arthritis in his spine.'

'Sclerosis,' said Luke, who had had an aunt who had suffered from it.

'If you say so,' Billy replied. 'Anyway, he can't work no more; he's already worn himself out with labor.'

'And Boston?'

'You don't know Boston Sears. I heard him ask you if you had heard of him. I suppose he wanted you to say that you knew him by reputation. Boston Sears has never lifted anything in his life, except for raising a six-gun to do his dirty work.'

3

They watched a flight of doves winging its way across the coloring sky headed for some secret watering place. Then Billy rose from his rock and told Luke, 'It's time we got to work. They'll hear that our picks aren't biting.'

It was warm but not excruciatingly hot when they started to work. Billy Rafferty had shed his shirt before entering the shallow declivity to begin work. His young muscles were taut and ropy. When he began to use his pick Luke could see how they had gotten that way. His pick rose and fell, flashed in the faint sunlight, striking rock and breaking it free of the cave's walls. Luke knew he was a strong enough man, but after half an hour of using his pick his body had begun to throb with exhaustion, his old injuries seeming to cramp his nerves. His ribs were especially

painful. Billy worked on, his motions machine-like.

Billy recognized the slowing pace of Luke's work.

'Take a break,' he said. 'We all know that you've been hurt.'

'Thanks,' Luke said, feeling old beside this muscular, healthy young man. He leaned his pick against the wall of the cave. 'Want to join me?'

Billy shook his head. 'Not until I get another barrowful. This will never be finished if I take a break anytime I want.'

'What are we trying to finish, exactly?' Luke Walsh asked. 'What is the purpose of this shaft? I mean, I know it's supposed to be a mine of some sort — but why here?'

Now Billy did lower his pick. He smiled. 'I believe I will take a break with you, Luke.' Sweat was trickling from Luke's forehead into his eyes, stinging them. Billy, in contrast, seemed dry and unaware of the heat which had been building in the airless chamber.

Billy walked out with him into the open where the dry wind lifted from the desert floor. He nodded at a nearby upturned wheelbarrow. 'Do you think you're up to loading that and hauling away the tailings? It's easier work; it's what I usually do when I need a break. You can see that cleft over there. That's where I've been dumping the rock.'

'I'll give it a try. I'm sorry, Billy. I just don't have my usual strength.'

'It'll come back. With Susan's cooking.'

'Who is the older woman with the steel-gray hair? I thought maybe she was the cook and housekeeper.'

Billy laughed out loud. 'That is Emma. She is Boston Sears's mother. She has decided her life's work is done. She doesn't do anything up here but take up space.'

Luke nodded. He remembered the woman's refusal to bring food and water to him, saying she had not been brought up to be a nurse. Well, it didn't matter much, he supposed. He

had just been wondering, trying to get a handle on who these people were and their relationship to each other. One thing was important: no one had explained why they were digging this shaft, far away from civilization, at this remote and primitive site. Billy Rafferty explained as they rested.

'It all goes back to Clancy Gunn,' Billy told him. He nodded his head toward the old mine near which they were working. 'Gunn took a fair amount of gold out of that mine years ago. Hauled it all the way to Tucson. Never told anyone where he was digging it.'

'But people found out?'

'Yes, someone trailed him back out here, I suppose. Old Gunn was killed, or simply died — no one knows. It didn't matter as it turned out; the mine was dry, the gold vein stripped bare of ore. Useless. But then . . . ' Billy said. Luke encouraged him with a nod. He could see that the blond kid was watching the long ascending path to make sure no one was coming up to ask why the work had stopped.

'Go on.'

'After Gunn was gone, someone found a diagram . . . ' Billy faltered.

'A map?'

'A map is when it's above ground, isn't it? Like a chart is just when you're on the sea — I don't know — call it what you will. A map that showed why Gunn had quit digging. The seam had met some sort of break in the earth, a place where it had been shifted by ancient forces and lifted up so that the seam broke off. The map made it clear that there was more to the gold vein but a new shaft would have to be dug. There was no way to bring more equipment out here and hire more men, and anyway Gunn had died. Somehow Boston Sears came upon the old map. He knew the legend of the gold of Gun Hill but couldn't figure how to make it profitable, either,' Billy said. 'He started 'recruiting' men.'

'Meaning?'

'If he were a seaman, you'd call it shanghaiing,' Billy explained. 'I'd call it slavery. You're not the first man to find himself laboring on Gun Hill, and I don't suppose you'll be the last.'

'What happened to the others?' Luke asked with real concern.

'Two men died — they were unfit for the job. Drunks picked up in a saloon alleyway. They didn't last a week. A couple of others made a break for it on foot across the desert. You can guess their fate.'

A gravelly voice echoed up the hill toward them.

'Hey, Billy, what are you two doing up there?'

'We'd better get back to work. There's the shovel and the barrow. Help me out as best you can.'

The day wore on, growing warm and then smoky-hot. Luke shoveled the tailings of Billy's work into the wheelbarrow and dumped it where he had been told to do so. The work was no easier than the pick work had been for his tired body, which ached with each overloaded barrow, but he had given these men his promise, and besides there was nothing else to do. What? Make a run for it on foot across a trackless desert, without water or supplies of any sort? Beneath the searing sun he would be dead within a mile, even if he were in healthy shape.

There was nothing to do but labor on. The sweat ran freely from his body now; back and chest dripped with it. He felt his shoulders, and probably his legs, could not hold up much longer.

At noon there was a pleasant, almost joyous surprise.

The seemingly tireless Billy came out of the shaft and whistled to Luke. The kid pointed his finger down the trail and Luke, mopping his forehead, looked that way to see Susan Rafferty making her way up the rough path, carrying a canteen and a bucket, which presumably held their lunch, trudging her way toward them. Her expression when she arrived, made it clear that she was tired, but she managed a smile for Luke.

'Hard going?' she asked.

'It hasn't been easy,' Luke Walsh answered. He tugged at his shirt to vent himself.

'Frank said to tell you that you can knock off any time you want,' Susan told him. 'We all know your condition.'

'What did Boston say?' Luke asked, having already acquired a distaste for and mistrust of Boston Sears.

'Boston isn't here. He's making another ride into Tucson. He thinks the work is going too slowly — even with you here. He's gone looking for new recruits.'

'To hire new men?' Luke asked, accepting a ham sandwich on thick-sliced sourdough bread from Susan's small hand. He seated himself on a rock which had now grown sun-hot, winced, and waited for an answer.

'To 'recruit them', I said. I don't know how he goes about it,' Susan said.

'Or care?'

'Of course I care!' she snapped, 'but what am I to do about it?'

Billy sat on a nearby rock, shirtless, eating his sandwich in silence. He looked deliberately away from their conversation.

'I thank you for the sandwich and the water,' Luke said. 'It's done me more good than you can imagine.'

'It's nothing,' Susan murmured.

'Susan?' Luke said, taking her wrist as she began to start away, 'how did Boston get mixed up in all this? I thought the land belonged to your father.'

'It does, but as you must have noticed Frank is not fit enough to do much work. Boston showed up with this hand-drawn map, presumably made by Clancy Gunn, that showed how the old vein of ore could be reached by digging a shaft higher up the ridge. Boston had a little cash money and so Father took him in as a partner.'

'I see. I wonder where Boston got the

map — from Gunn himself?'

'I don't know,' Susan replied uneasily.

'Because it's been said that Gunn might have been murdered,' Luke said.

'I wouldn't know about that,' Susan said, casting a dark glance in her cousin's direction. Lifting her voice a little, she said, 'Some people talk too much about things they know nothing about.'

'All right,' Luke said, recognizing a stalemate when he met one. Susan gathered the leftover implements and the pail she had brought.

'I was supposed to tell you, Luke — you'll be taking up new lodgings tonight, sleeping out in the bunkhouse with Billy.'

'All right,' Luke said. He had not seen the bunkhouse; he presumed it was the old log structure standing at the base of the rocky hill behind the main house. 'I guess I won't be seeing you much, then.'

'I'll still bring you water and your

lunch, still cook you your breakfast and supper,' Susan said, her cheeks seeming to grow a little pinker. Maybe it was just the heat of the day which had risen even as they spoke that caused it. Luke stood and watched Susan's slender back as she made her way down the rough path.

He went back to work, loading the barrow and hauling away rocks, while Billy chipped away at the face of the shaft walls. It grew hotter and Luke was having trouble catching his breath as sweat streamed down his body and soaked his shirt. His body was just too weak yet for this kind of work. Seeing Billy working his rhythmic, seemingly tireless way, Luke staggered toward the blond kid and said with a kind of shame, 'I'm sorry, Billy. I've had it.'

'All right then,' Billy said without pausing in his work. 'We knew you were kind of beat up. Go on over to the bunkhouse and take a rest. You can get back to it tomorrow. The lower first bunk on the right is mine; feel free to take any of the others. There's a water barrel inside beside the door. I'll see you about supper time.'

Luke felt like apologizing further to the hard-working kid, but Billy seemed to take no offense at his leaving early. Looking at the work that had been done, Luke couldn't see that they had made much progress at all. But, he supposed, men in search of gold may not be in a rush, but they are tenacious — especially when the labor is not their own.

He slipped once going down the rock trail and landed hard on his tailbone. Automatically he looked around, hoping no one had noticed this further embarrassment. But the day was still and hot. He sat for a moment before he rose, looking out across the long desert where nothing lived, little grew, where no water stood. A man on a horse could escape, he supposed, if he took water along. But in Luke's situation, where would he be riding but back into the arms of the law? Maybe Gun Hill wouldn't be so bad after he got used to the work. Billy seemed to like him well enough — and there was Susan Rafferty.

He got to his feet and started down the steeply sloped hill toward the bunkhouse. The outbuilding was small, but neatly ordered. Three two-bunk beds were there, one on each side, the third against the back wall. That wall had a narrow window cut into the wooden walls, and Luke liked the idea of having some extra light, so he took the top bunk against the far wall and stretched out wearily on the thin mattress. At least he was out of the sun, though the almost airless confines of the outbuilding were nearly stifling despite the fact that Luke had left the door open upon entering.

He had laid his head down in worse places. He closed his eyes and managed to fall off to sleep in a few minutes while the silent day crept past.

About an hour later a sound from the doorway caused Luke's eyes to flicker open. A bewildered-looking young man about twenty years old stood there, his silhouette stark against the glare off the sunlit hills behind him.

'Is this the place?' the young stranger asked as Luke Walsh swung his legs to the side of his upper bunk, rubbing at his eyes.

'That depends on what place you're looking for,' Luke replied.

'They said I could find myself somewhere to sleep out back. Is this it?'

'This is it,' Luke said, leaping down to the floor. 'Bring in your gear if you have any.'

'No, I don't.' The younger man stepped out of the sunlight and Luke got a good look at him. He was tall, wiry with thick yellow hair that resembled mown hay. His chin receded slightly and he had buck teeth. 'Are you in charge here?' he asked Luke.

'Not hardly. How did you come to make your way here?' Luke asked, clambering up on to his bunk again.

'Well, sir,' the kid said, sitting on the

bunk opposite Billy Rafferty's, looking exhausted and sun-beaten. 'I was on my way to Crater — do you know where that is? Most folks don't.' Luke gave a negative shake of his head. 'I was told I could find work there. That fool mule of mine busted his leg and I had to put him down. Then . . . I started walking and realized I wasn't going to make it. Some folks who live up here were passing by and offered me a job and a place to stay for a while. You bet I accepted! What about you?'

'Pretty much the same story,' Luke Walsh said.

'Have they treated you all right up here?' the kid asked, glancing toward the door.

'So far, yes,' Luke had to admit but he didn't like the feel of the place. It seemed . . . secretive. 'I didn't get your name,' he said to the younger man.

'It's Richard Dockery. Dick Dockery.' He smiled. 'Most folks back home just call me Tick-Tock.'

'Mine's Luke Walsh. There's nothing

else to be done around here before supper time. Choose a bunk and stretch out. That's what I'm going to do. You noticed the water barrel, didn't you?'

'I sure did,' Dockery said, rising to walk that way and dip out water with a tin cup. He had three cups, then lay back on his bed. Tick-Tock was asleep before Luke could fall back into the land of dreams.

Both men were sleeping soundly when Billy Rafferty tramped into the bunkhouse; both were awakened. Beyond Billy, Luke could see that the land had darkened. A purple twilight hung over the barren hills.

'Come on, men!' Billy called out cheerfully. 'You don't want to miss supper. Time to wash up and fill our stomachs.'

They washed outside at a barrel used for that purpose, passing a bar of yellow lye soap from hand to hand. To the west, above the long desert, Luke could see that the sky still held color and light. The playa shimmered with gold and violet hues.

'Everybody ready?' Billy asked, turning his cuffs down. He and Tick-Tock had already introduced themselves. Billy welcomed the new man as he had welcomed Luke: pleasantly, almost eager for his company.

As they made their way toward the big house, Billy said to Luke, 'You'll be expected to put in a full work day tomorrow.'

'I'll do my best.'

'Tick-Tock,' Billy told the new arrival, 'we want you to at least come up and take a look around the project.'

'I can work,' Tick-Tock said firmly.

'All the better. We usually don't expect a new man to put in a full day on his first shift.'

'I . . . I can do it,' Tick-Tock said. His voice was quavering. Luke decided that Tick-Tock had only recently learned to control a constant stammer. Billy looped an arm over Tick-Tock's shoulder and smiled.

'Of course you can, but tomorrow

we're going to take it a little easy on you. We don't want to kill off our new-hires!' Billy laughed, but the sound seemed to Luke's ears to be forced joviality. After all, it was Billy Rafferty who had told him that at least three men had already died on Gun Hill — or in trying to make their escape from it. He doubted that Boston Sears cared much if any of his laborers died. There were always more to be found, picked up on the desert or dragged from the alleys behind saloons.

Yes, Boston Sears had a talent for recruiting men to work in his mine.

The three men approached the house by the back way, where three thorny mesquite trees grew, etched darkly against the fading sky. Luke hated these plants. He kept his arms tucked in, not wanting to be bitten by their barbs. They looked pretty enough in this light, but they reminded Luke of some women he had known — better seen and admired from a distance.

They tramped through the back door

59

and in to the kitchen. Luke looked around hopefully but futilely for Susan; she was not there. They passed through the kitchen, Billy leading the way into the dining room. Luke saw immediately that a second trestle table had been set up there. Boston had company visiting. A lady in a yellow dress sat at the head of the table, her eyes sparkling, her dark hair sleek and glossy.

It was Dee Dee Bright.

4

His eyes met Dee Dee's, but both turned their gazes quickly away. Susan came in wearing an apron, looking a little frazzled and red from the heat of the kitchen stove. She first served the fancier table where Frank Rafferty, Boston Sears, his mother Emma, Dee Dee Bright and a stranger in a black suit sat. Somehow the man's attire was not trail-dusty, but neatly pressed. Because of Dee Dee's presence, Luke Walsh assumed that this man was probably Dee Dee's lover, the infamous Virgil Sly.

Sly seemed to be a little shorter than Luke, and his nose was prominent and arched. He had his dark hair slicked back and parted in the middle. He had a razor-thin mustache clinging to his upper lip. He wasn't really a prepossessing figure but Luke, looking that way, studied the man's brown eyes. There seemed to be no light at all in them. He gave the impression of a man who would shoot you giving it no more thought than to squashing a bug.

It was now their table's turn to be served. Susan delivered a dish of hot corn bread and filled their bowls with beef stew. Neither Billy nor Tick-Tock wasted any time before digging in, Billy grabbing squares of cornbread with both hands. Well, Billy Rafferty did work hard, and Tick Tock was probably still half starved after his desert trek. Luke had a sudden loss of appetite as he watched Susan bustling around from table to kitchen and back again. Frank Rafferty did not give his daughter so much as a nod of approval.

Emma Sears ate as rapidly as Billy and Tick-Tock, but managed to criticize the food at the same time. Virgil Sly and Boston Sears had fallen into a close conversation at the end of the table. Dee Dee's eyes flickered toward Luke once in a while. He ate in silence. There was too much going on around here, much of it furtive and all of it a little unsettling.

By the time Luke had finished his meal Billy and Tick-Tock were long done. Billy stretched his arms widely and said, 'Me, I'm ready to get some sleep.'

'S-so am I,' Tick-Tock said, keeping his eyes away from the finer folks at the other table.

'Ready to go, Luke?' Billy asked. Luke Walsh thought he saw Virgil Sly's eyes flicker toward them as his name was spoken.

'I suppose we'd better,' Luke said, placing his napkin aside. 'Shouldn't someone help Susan clear these tables?'

'We all have our own jobs,' Billy said. 'You won't see her with a pick and shovel.'

'I suppose not,' Luke murmured. He rose from the table, feeling somehow guilty, and followed the other two workers toward the back door. Passing through the kitchen he lagged and held

63

back as Billy and Tick-Tock went out. Susan was sitting alone at a small table, eating. Her hair was across her forehead and into her eyes. The heat in the kitchen was oppressive.

'Billy said you didn't need any help,' Luke said, beginning an apology.

'Oh, no!' she snapped. 'I don't need any help. Let's just start a boarding house.'

'Sorry,' Luke muttered. He started toward the back door. Susan was suddenly on her feet. She reached for his arm. 'Let's step outside for a minute.'

They went out into the yard, if it could be called that. Hard-pan soil where nothing could grow except the thorny mesquite. It was still hot outside, but nothing like it had been in the furnace of the kitchen. Luke even imagined he could feel a faint fitful breeze, no stronger than the brushing of feathers against his flesh.

'I didn't mean to sound peevish,' Susan said. Adjusting her skirt and apron she sat down on the wooden step that led into the house.

'That's all right,' Luke said, standing in front of her as the starlight took over the long desert skies. 'I know how hard it must be to rise and fix breakfast for everyone, then make dinner and supper, serving all the food with barely enough time to wash the dishes and scrub the pots and pans in between.'

Susan waved a dismissive hand in the air. 'It's all right. I suppose I can handle it. You know,' she said, 'I used to not mind a bit, when Father, Cousin Billy and I were up here alone. I knew Father couldn't do much work and also that Billy was working all day. But after Boston Sears and his mother got here . . . ' Her voice trailed off.

'Why did Boston come up here?' Luke glanced around. 'It doesn't seem that he'd have any reason to.'

'Two reasons. You know, of course, about the map to the mine.' She said this as if in mockery.

'You don't think there's anything to that?'

'Oh, I don't know. No one knows where it came from or who drew it.'

'I was told that it was Clancy Gunn himself.'

Susan shrugged. 'Maybe it was,' she admitted, 'but no one knows. Clancy's long dead now and can't be asked.'

'Your father bought the claim from Clancy?'

'Shortly before his passing. Clancy had to talk up the claim, of course, to get Father to use his life savings to buy it. Frank had the idea that he could find at least enough gold in the old mine to see that Billy and I would be taken care of after he was gone himself.'

'So when Boston Sears showed up with the map, it encouraged your father more.'

'Of course! Even though he was forced to let Boston have half of the claim.'

'I see — I think,' Luke said. 'You said there were two reasons Boston Sears showed up here. What was the other one?'

'Simple,' Susan said, rising from the step. 'Look around you. Can you think of a better place to hide out from the law?' She paused another minute.

'Do you know that girl?' Susan asked abruptly.

'What girl do you mean?' Luke asked, taken aback.

'The only other girl in the house. The one in the fancy dress. I saw you two looking at each other.'

'We've met — in Tucson,' Luke answered weakly.

Susan studied him by starlight, shook her head, and then she slipped back into the house. Emma Sears was calling to her, demanding more coffee. Luke's mouth twisted a little as he turned and started toward the bunkhouse. He didn't make it far.

The shadow of a man emerged from behind the thinner shadows cast by the mesquite and before Luke could react, a fist was driven into Luke's belly. A second blow landed on Luke's already damaged ribs and he folded up, gasping for air. He tried to fight back, but his attacker was only a moving shadow in the darkness. A solid uppercut caught Luke under the jaw and he staggered away, his back coming to rest against the thorny base of a mesquite tree, his head ringing.

The shadow said in a hoarse whisper, 'I'm warning you to stay away from that girl, or you'll get worse.'

Then as Luke watched skyward, trying to catch his breath, the shadow moved away and blended into the darkness of the night.

Well, he had been warned, but he didn't know who had warned him. Or what girl the stranger had been talking about. There was no way to estimate the size or bulk of the man in the darkness. Luke only knew that he packed a powerful punch. He got to his feet, shaking his head, and looked back at the dim light from the kitchen.

Had someone seen him talking to

Susan? He wondered if Boston Sears had his own eye on the pretty little blonde. That could be. It could also be that Virgil Sly had seen something pass between him and Dee Dee. It could even be that she had told him something she shouldn't have.

Luke staggered toward the bunkhouse, holding his injured ribs. He supposed it didn't matter. He would have few occasions to see either of the women again, even if he wanted to. His head was ringing, his ribs ached. The thorns of the mesquite had raked his back. He couldn't have been too pretty when he reentered the bunkhouse. The eyes of Billy and Tick-Tock lifted to study him.

'That took a while,' Billy said. He was cocked up on one elbow in his bunk. 'We were starting to worry about you.'

Luke only muttered, then made his way toward his bed, stumbling a little as he went. Looking up at it he wondered why he had chosen an upper bunk.

With considerable effort which must have been obvious to both Billy Rafferty and Tick-Tock, he clambered on to his bunk and fell back, his arm over his eyes. Neither of the other two men asked a question. Luke figured it was not that they didn't care; they simply did not want to know what had happened.

After a while the pain subsided and he was able to sleep as time passed and the moon rose through the skies over Gun Hill.

★   ★   ★

He awoke to sounds of movement, to a heavy scraping of an object against the floor. Day was dawning over the hills; it was time to rise. Opening his eyes he glanced toward the doorway and saw Tick-Tock and Billy positioning a heavy round table in the center of the bunkhouse. Luke climbed down and went forward to join them. Billy smiled.

'This is where we eat from now on,

boys,' Billy announced.

'As long as we eat,' Tick-Tock said.

'Oh, we'll eat. Men who don't eat can't work. What about it, Luke?' he asked.

'Makes no difference to me.' Luke shrugged. 'Any reason for it, though?'

'The extra table was taking up too much room in the house, Uncle Frank said, and it'd have to be put up and taken down for every meal.'

'That makes sense, I suppose,' Luke had to admit.

'Sure!' Billy agreed, slapping Luke on the back. 'I'd rather not have to share space with the others anyway — although I didn't mind having a look at that new woman, Sly's girlfriend.'

'It's probably best to stay as far away from her, and from Virgil Sly as possible,' Luke commented.

'You say that as if you knew them,' Billy said, his smile fading.

'We've met,' Luke answered, but refused to be drawn any further in conversation.

By the time they had all finished dressing, Susan arrived carrying a heavy tray. 'What do you think of the new arrangement, Cousin?' Billy asked cheerfully. Susan didn't smile in return.

'I think it gives me one more long trip to make at mealtimes,' she said, placing the heavy tray down. 'Not even a tablecloth?'

'No one here minds,' Billy said. 'All these boys care about is filling their stomachs.'

From the pocket of her apron Susan extracted a handful of knives, forks and spoons. She let them clatter down on to the table. 'I'll be back with a pot of coffee. Now I get to boil two for every meal,' she complained.

She turned sharply and walked away, the heels on her small boots clicking against the floor.

'Makes me feel sorry for the girl,' Tick-Tock said.

'Sorry enough to keep you from eating?' Billy asked.

Tick-Tock grinned. 'No, sir! I don't know anything can make me that sorrowful.'

Luke began to eat in silence, watching the door for Susan's return. He had not failed to notice that she had not given him so much as a glance. Was this about Dee Dee Bright? What did Susan know or guess about their past? It didn't matter, but he had wanted to make a good impression on the blonde girl.

Maybe he was imagining things, Luke thought as he continued to eat. The ham was good but a little raw, as if it had not been smoked long enough. Billy must have seen the expression on his face.

'That's peccary,' Billy told him. 'Wild boar. There's a lot of them around here. The meat's hardly as sweet as a Virginia ham, but we have to use what we have out here.'

'Tastes fine to me,' Tick-Tock said. Luke was starting to think that anything he could fit in his mouth tasted fine to

Tick-Tock. He wondered if the kid came from a background of extreme poverty. Susan returned with a gallon pot of coffee just as they were finishing up. She placed it down on the table, gripping it with two hand towels.

'If there's any coffee left when you're finished, don't toss it out. You'll likely be having it for lunch today — if I have the time to make you any lunch.'

'Sounds like they're really working you, Cousin,' Billy said.

'Extra rooms to clean, beds to make, waiting on the two fine ladies — yes, you could say they are working me a bit.'

'Maybe the female guest will volunteer to help out,' Tick-Tock said. Susan's mouth grew tight.

'I'll not hold my breath,' she said. 'Her kind doesn't think work includes things like cleaning and cooking.'

Susan went out again, and again, Luke noticed, she had not once looked his way. She was mad at him, all right. He pushed the thought aside, there being nothing he could do about it anyway. Billy was talking:

'We've got a wagonload of timber out there, boys. It's all got to be carried up by hand — no wagon can climb the road to the mine. We're not in need of the timbers yet. We're not far enough along to have to be worried about shoring up. But we will need them. I'm thinking we should make two trips up this morning, carrying what we can. If we do the same every day, it'll eventually be there for use when we do need it.'

'Have you any experience at shoring, Billy?' Luke asked.

Billy shook his head, 'No, but I have been into Gunn's old mine quite often. I figure just to try to do it the way he did. The old mine hasn't caved in yet.'

The thought made Luke a little uneasy; he thought he saw the same concern in Tick-Tock's eyes. The rock up there seemed utterly solid, but there could always be a cave-in. Luke had no wish to be caught under one.

Billy was smiling. He placed his napkin aside and rose, 'Don't worry, boys. Who knows, maybe Boston Sears will bring us a mining engineer before we get to that point.' He planted his hat and handed out work gloves to them. 'Ready to go?'

The morning didn't start out well. Some of the wood was nothing more than pole corral stock, others were heavy twelve-by-twelve timbers, badly weathered and rough with huge splinters. It took both Luke and Tick-Tock to hoist one of these from the pile where they had been dumped from the wagon, then haul it up the steep, rock-strewn path to the cave. They fell more than once. Tick-Tock sat muttering small curses beside the timber they had dropped on a steep incline. He was holding his knee. Luke could see blood on Tick-Tock's leg through the rip he had torn in his twill trousers.

'I didn't know it was going to be this rough,' Tick-Tock said. Luke only nodded and helped him to his feet when he was ready to continue. It was just past dawn; a ground fog was lying in the low ravines. Luke didn't have the heart to tell Tick-Tock that they hadn't even begun working yet.

Achieving the flat they dumped the timber on a small pile of pole logs that Billy had begun. Billy told them — 'Better keep this stuff separated by size. It'll make it easier on down the road.'

After shifting the heavy timber to one side Luke went to stand beside Billy, taking in deep breaths of the relatively cool morning air as he looked out again at the intimidating wasteland beyond.

'Same thing as yesterday?' Luke asked.

'Same thing as yesterday, tomorrow, every day,' Billy said with one of his habitual smiles. 'We'd better let Tick-Tock use the barrow today, don't you think? Are you ready for some pick-swinging?'

'It sounds like I'd better be,' Luke

answered, tugging up his work gloves.

'You'll be fine,' Billy said, slapping Luke on the back as he had a habit of doing. Billy began whistling as they made their way to the mouth of the mine. Luke had to ask him:

'How is it you're always able to maintain a good mood, Billy?'

'What else do I have to keep me going?' Billy Rafferty asked, his face momentarily serious. 'Let's get to it. You show Tick-Tock where we dump the tailings.'

They began work. Billy was his usual rhythmic self with the pick. Luke started slowly, but gradually his muscles loosened and he found himself swinging the implement with more ease. Nothing like Billy's pace, but enough for him to feel he was contributing. Until somewhere around noon.

The heat in the shaft was stifling. His entire body was soaked in perspiration. The pick seemed to weigh twenty pounds more. It was difficult even to breathe as the rock dust clogged the mine. Luke retied his bandanna bandit-style so that it covered mouth and nostrils. It did little good against the pervasive dust. His eyes were stinging from his own sweat and from the dust hanging in the air. It had to be over a hundred degrees outside, hotter in the shaft. They worked on.

The only break in the work came when Tick-Tock, pushing the two-wheeled barrow into the tunnel, had to be given room to shovel the stone before carting it away. Luke was gasping for breath, his shoulder muscles feeling fiery with the exertion when Billy at last called a halt to the work.

'Nearly time for lunch,' Billy Rafferty said, and Luke thought that he had never heard such wonderful words. Leaning their pick-handles against the wall of the cave, they made their way over the remaining rubble and went out into the desert-hot day.

The sun shimmered down against the wide white playa. It beat against their skulls and exposed flesh. There was an occasional gust of air, but the wind, blowing hot off the desert, did nothing to cool them although it did dry Luke's body. They retreated to the heated shade of the rocks beside the mine opening and sat down to wait for Susan.

Poor girl, Luke thought: there was no respite for her.

'Do you ever think about just pulling out?' he asked Billy. The blond man shrugged.

'And go where? Besides, I owe my Uncle Frank. As long as he stays, I stay.'

'The same goes for Susan?'

'He's her father! Besides,' Billy said, lowering his voice. 'Susan has no place else to go either — none of us does, I expect.'

Tick-Tock had noticed that the others had quit working, so he came toward them, pushing his empty barrow. 'What is it?' he asked.

'Lunch,' Billy told him. Tick-Tock nodded and placed the barrow down. He sat on a nearby rock, mopping his brow with his bandanna. He looked much worse than Luke felt. Tick-Tock's face was ghostly white, his movements were uncertain. The sun had gotten to him. When he sagged on to the rock, he had to brace himself with both hands. He was on the very verge of heatstroke. Billy and Luke exchanged a look.

'That's it for you,' Billy told Tick-Tock. 'For today, at least. Have your lunch and then go back to the bunkhouse.

'Thanks,' Tick-Tock said, lifting pitiable eyes to Billy Rafferty. 'I can work on if you need me.'

'We will need you — but no more today,' Billy replied. 'I told you the new man usually only works a half-day. This kind of work takes some getting used to. You'll come back tomorrow and be twice as much help as you could possibly be this afternoon.'

'Thanks,' Tick-Tock said again. He was doubled over at the waist and for a moment Luke thought he was going to be sick, but he straightened up again and reached for the canteen Billy was trying to hand him.

'Here she comes!' Billy announced, and Luke glanced down the rocky slope watching as Susan struggled upward, slipping now and then, lunch bucket in her hands. Luke felt a pang of pity: what had Susan done to deserve such a life?

Lunch was again ham sandwiches — peccary sandwiches, Luke supposed. As Susan had warned them, she had brought along the remains of their morning coffee. She had taken the time to reheat it, but it was getting pretty strong and bitter. Nevertheless, the meal was welcome. Billy ate eagerly, not bothering to talk. Tick-Tock had trouble getting started. He was obviously suffering from the heat and exertion. Eventually he took a small bite of his sandwich and began slowly chewing.

Luke's eyes were on Susan as she collected the tin cups and pot, the lunch bucket. Again she had failed to speak so much as a word to him. She waved a not-so-cheery hand to the men and started down the rugged trail again.

Billy told Tick-Tock again, 'Whenever you want to go, just follow her along.'

'I think I will,' Tick-Tock said, rising unsteadily. They watched him stagger off toward the head of the trail and begin making his way down the slope. Luke finished his sandwiches, drank some water from the canteen and stood looking at the red bluff that loomed over them.

'Do you think there's really any gold in here?' Luke asked. Billy gave Luke one of his easy smiles.

'Guess we won't know until we find it,' Billy answered. 'The thing is, my Uncle Frank does. He's staked everything he ever had on it. So, me, I keep on digging.' He shrugged. Luke nodded. He had turned to look out across the wide desert again. Billy must have seen the expression in his eyes. He rose and told Luke:

'Don't even think about it, my friend. There's no way out of here unless you've got a gun and a good horse. Boston Sears makes sure of that.'

5

As dusk was beginning to settle across the desert again, Luke Walsh lay, exhausted, on his bunk. Tick-Tock had remained asleep as they tramped in from the mine. Likely he would remain asleep until morning. He had had a pretty rough first day. Billy had gone to the big house to speak with his Uncle Frank about something.

Unable to relax his weary body, Luke lay awake thinking as the skies purpled outside. His eyelids closed, and as his breathing slowed he was able to begin to doze off. He half-heard the small shuffling footsteps outside and then a light, tentative rapping on the frame of the open door.

Luke couldn't see across the room in the darkness. He knew that Tick-Tock was still deep in exhausted sleep and that Billy had not yet returned from his visit with his uncle, so, giving a small grunt of resignation, he swung his feet from his bunk, turned his body and dropped to the floor. He could see a few bright stars shining through the notch in the bulk of the dark hills beyond and little else. Who . . . ?

He reached the doorway to find her standing to one side. Dee Dee Bright was waiting in the night. 'Can I come in?' she whispered. 'I need to talk to you.'

'No,' Luke said sternly, glancing around to see who else might be roaming about.

'Please!' Dee Dee said, moving nearer to take the fabric of his shirtsleeve in her fingers. 'It's really important — I can't tell you how important it is.' Her eyes were star-bright; a mysterious, agreeable scent filled his nostrils. She was wearing a midnight-blue dress of some silky material, but no hat. Nor was her hair pinned up. It cascaded in a dark flow across her shoulders. Luke shook his head.

'It's not safe for you to come in. Billy will be back soon, and there's another man asleep in here.'

'Then come outside with me. For just a minute, Luke. I'm begging you.'

'I don't feel like getting beaten up again,' Luke said, removing his shirtsleeve from her grasp.

'When did that happen? Who did it?' Dee Dee asked in an excited whisper.

'Last night. It must have been Virgil Sly, don't you think?'

'Why would he . . . oh.' Her eyes turned down.

'Yes, 'oh'. What have you told him about us?'

'Not the whole truth,' Dee Dee said. 'But, Luke, it wasn't Virgil, believe me. He doesn't use his fists to solve his problems. If it were Virgil Sly you'd be lying dead right now with a bullet hole in you.'

'That's a comfort,' Luke muttered.

Dee Dee now looked around nervously. 'Can we move away from the doorway?' she asked.

'That's a good idea, although I don't see what we could possibly have to talk about.'

She took his hand and tugged him into deeper darkness.

About fifty feet from the bunkhouse she stopped and faced him again. It was a good thing they had moved, for a minute later Luke saw Billy Rafferty arrive at the building, scrape his boots and step inside, lighting a lantern.

'Now then,' Luke asked, still irritable, 'what is it that's so important?'

'I want you to get me out of here, Luke.'

Luke Walsh studied her hopeful eyes in disbelief. She had waited for her outlaw lover to return and rescue her, had tricked Luke into killing the Tucson marshal to facilitate their escape, and now she wanted to leave Sly?

'I don't think I can help you, Dee Dee. I don't see how. What's happened?'

'When we arrived here Virgil told me that we were just going to rest the horses for a while. I didn't know one of the old Red Butte gang was living here.'

'Boston Sears?'

'Yes, that's the name he's using now. He and Virgil have had their heads together.'

'I've seen them talking,' Luke said, wondering if that was a part of the reason they were eating in the bunkhouse these days: the bandits did not wish to be overheard.

'So have I, at all hours,' Dee Dee said. 'They shut up whenever I happen to be around. But I've heard enough to know that they're planning something. One night they were sitting around with a sheet of paper, drawing plans or a map on it. I was sent away immediately. Virgil tries to calm me and tells me that we're still heading for Mexico, but that it will take a little while. He's not taking me. I know it,' Dee Dee almost whined.

'I thought that you told me he had all the money he would ever need.'

'Did I? I don't know — maybe he was lying to me; maybe he lost it gambling. I just know that something very bad is going to happen and that I'll never get to Mexico, not with Virgil Sly, at least.' Her eyes recovered that pleading look. She looked up at him in the near-darkness.

'You have to help me, Luke. You did it before.'

'And look where that's gotten me,' he growled. Taking a deep breath, he said, 'There's no way out of here, Dee Dee. Not without horses and a gun.'

'I can get you some guns. I saw a rifle and a Colt in a pantry — they might even be yours!'

'They probably are,' Luke said. 'Then all we would need is two horses, some full canteens, a plan of escape and all the luck in the world.'

'You'll at least consider it then?' Dee Dee said with excitement. She had failed to understand the sarcasm in Luke's reply, wrapped up as she was in her own scheming. He didn't try to say any more to dissuade her. Every minute he spent with Dee Dee was risking jeopardy. She was much closer now, practically leaning against him. Neutrally, he told her:

'I consider everything.' He added quite seriously, 'It wouldn't hurt a bit if you could get your hands on those guns and hide them somewhere.'

'I can do that. I think I can,' she said eagerly. Then she kissed him, one of those soft, moist kisses Luke recalled so vividly during his lonely nights, but those times were past and there was only the future to think about.

If a man lets the same woman fool him twice in the same way, then he is indeed a fool. But, Luke reflected as Dee Dee turned and walked away, holding her skirts high, men are fools, making the same mistake endlessly when it comes to the temptations of a woman. He gave her a moment and then started back toward the bunkhouse where the lantern burned low, lighting the hard-packed ground in front of the open door.

He reached the door at almost the

same moment Susan Rafferty did.

'Who was that I saw running back toward the house?' she asked in a prickly tone. Her hands were holding a heavy tray. Luke offered, without speaking, to take it, but she hunched her shoulders in refusal.

'I didn't see anyone,' he lied. Susan gave a little sniff as if he had just confirmed all of her suspicions about him, then went in to place the tray on the table where Billy and Tick-Tock had already seated themselves in the wooden chairs, awaiting their meal.

'Thanks, Cousin,' Billy said cheerfully.

'Yes, thank you, miss,' Tick-Tock chimed in. Luke said nothing, figuring that Susan would only take it badly. She had already made up her mind about him. That was now clear. There was nothing he could say to her to convince her otherwise. He and Dee Dee were lovers in Susan's mind. Damnit, she was half right!

Luke turned a chair and sat to the

table. He ate sullenly. The meal was what seemed to be some of the leftover beef stew with a few potatoes added to it, and fresh cornbread. It was nothing to complain about, and the three ate heartily. A few times Billy or Tick-Tock tried to start up a conversation with Luke, but he only nodded and continued to eat glumly.

Luke was back in his bunk before Susan returned to pick up the utensils and empty bowls. In the dim light of the bunkhouse she could not see his eyes fixed longingly on her. She did not glance in his direction, but scooped up what she had come for, wished Billy and Tick-Tock a good night and vanished into the night again.

Luke rolled over to face the wall, wondering about his unhappy fate and the way he himself had caused it.

In the morning, his body was not eager to rise. Billy had to come to his bunk to shake him awake.

'Breakfast is already set up,' he said. 'Better come and get your share before

Tick-Tock eats it all.'

Luke grunted an answer and sat up. He had no wish to face the day. Susan was still on his mind, had been in his broken dreams all through the night. Unhappy, sullen, he dressed and made his way to the table. There was a faint gleam of red-violet above the skyline to the east.

They were back to the timber pile half an hour later as the first yellow light of real dawn appeared in the sky over the hills and long shadows stretched out from the base of the bluff, like the mountain darkly yawning.

'How are you feeling this morning, Tick-Tock?' Billy asked as they staggered and stumbled upward with timbers over their shoulders.

'Better. All right, I guess,' Tick-Tock replied.

'Neither of you is in great shape yet. I think for today you and Luke should take turns picking and wheeling the barrow. It'll make it a little easier on both of you.'

'You're the boss,' Tick-Tock answered. Billy laughed in response.

'Am I? The boss of what?' For a moment a dark mood seemed to pass behind Billy's eyes. Luke saw it flash and then vanish in the blink of an eye as Billy Rafferty regained his good spirits. 'Good enough, boys,' he said, 'Drop the twelve-by-twelve with the others. I think I caught a splinter.' He removed his glove and began biting at his palm. After a bit he managed to extract an inch-long gray splinter from the flesh of his hand. He spat it out and squeezed blood from the wound.

'Nasty stuff, that,' Billy said, kicking a gray, weathered beam. 'I wish we had some new lumber to work with.'

'Who's that coming?' Tick-Tock said. He had been standing, looking out across the desert flats. Luke and Billy turned. Tick-Tock had raised a pointing finger. They all looked that way to see two men trailing in from the north. They rode steadily on, directly toward Gun Hill.

'I don't know,' Billy said, 'but they seem to know where they're headed.'

'Could be the law, after Virgil Sly or Boston Sears,' Luke suggested, although he hoped it was not so. He had no wish to confront any lawmen.

'Doubt it,' Billy said. 'Not coming from that direction. Besides there's only two of them — an unlikely posse. And they're not tracking anyone as you can see. They know exactly where they're going. They have to be friends of Sly or Boston. Maybe more members of that Red Butte gang. It doesn't matter much to us — let's get to work, boys.'

They began swinging their picks. As he worked, Luke remembered what Dee Dee had told him the night before. Boston and Virgil Sly had been hunched over a map or some sort of schematic, planning a caper. These must be two more of the men they had invited in to help them pull a big job. He could go no further with that line of thinking. No one could guess what the two outlaws had in mind, nor, as Billy had said, could it matter much to them.

With any luck, the outlaws would go off and get themselves shot up trying to rob a bank.

The work was no easier, no more difficult than it had been the day before. Meaning, it was torment under the desert sky, but Luke's muscles felt freer now and he worked through the morning without the exhaustion of previous days.

When they went outside at lunch-time, the faint, desultory desert breeze was a little more lively, if no cooler than previously. Luke could catch the scent of the juniper trees farther down the slope from where he sat. Tick-Tock approached them, smiling.

'How you feeling, Tick-Tock?' Billy asked.

'Not bad,' the buck-toothed kid said, removing his straw hat to sit in the warm shade. 'I'd still like to be somewhere else, though.'

'Well,' Billy said, 'if it's any comfort to you men, tomorrow's Sunday and we're off the job. Father doesn't hold with working on the Sabbath.'

That thought was enough to carry Luke through the afternoon, although he wondered what they could possibly do to occupy their time. Play cards? Sleep? Probably.

They were still waiting for Susan to bring their lunches, sipping from the canteen passed from hand to hand, when Tick-Tock observed, 'I hope it's something besides that pig meat again. You know, a man with a deer rifle and a shotgun could do himself some good around here. I've seen deer sign and noticed a lot of desert quail scurrying through the brush, and there's always doves.'

'You're right,' Billy agreed. 'We used to do more hunting. Now it's just the occasional tusked peccary that gets too bold and comes around the house that gets shot.'

'You agree with me?' Tick-Tock asked hopefully.

'Of course I do,' Billy answered.

'Now all we need is a man with a gun. Here comes Susan.'

Luke lifted his eyes almost dolefully to see the young woman in her light gingham dress laboring up the slope, bucket in her hands. The sight was depressing. He turned his eyes away, and kept from looking at Susan even as she handed out sandwiches which were of ground beef, left over from the stew meat, probably. It didn't matter. She talked to Billy for a few minutes and teased Tick-Tock a little, but said not a word to Luke Walsh.

When she had gone again, Billy asked, halfway through his sandwich, 'What did you do to that girl, Luke?'

'She's got a lot of imagination,' was all that Luke could think of to say. He finished his lunch in silence, returned to work in silence. Before knocking off at dusk, Luke eyed the shaft and had to admit they were making progress. Either the earth around them was not so solid now, making the going easier, or having two healthy men working at it was starting to yield results. Billy agreed with him as they placed their tools aside for the day.

'We're going to have to start thinking about using some of that timber to shore things up pretty soon.' Billy wore a satisfied expression as he wiped his forehead and throat with his bandanna. 'Uncle Frank will be pleased when I tell him, it's coming along.'

On the way down the steep trail Luke again began to wonder who the two newly arrived men were. They could have been only passers-by, but that seemed doubtful. No one came to Gun Hill except by deliberate plan.

Tick-Tock was in an unusually good mood, and Luke thought he knew why that was.

Sunday. There would be rest for the weary tomorrow. Six days a week working in the mine was enough to wear anyone down, even though they had not been on the job that long. How many more days would they be here? Luke had been willing to thank these men for saving his life, grateful to have a place to hide from the Tucson law. He had not given thought to escape until Dee Dee had approached him with the idea which sounded flimsy if not futile anyway. Yet he and Tick-Tock were prisoners here as surely as if they wore leg irons. In a way, so was Billy Rafferty; yet his imprisonment was a part of a family obligation. And what of Susan? What sort of life did she dream of for herself as she labored day and night?

Hers too was a family obligation for the man who had reared her and protected her all these years. But didn't there come a time when that must end? She was a virtual slave. Emma Sears seemed never to lift a finger to help her; it was certain that Dee Dee, who was unused to any sort of physical labor except for her specialty, would never offer to assist.

During his first dreadful day on Gun Hill, Tick-Tock had confided to Luke that he was ready to make a break for it and get on his way to Crater, where he had intended to ride all along. Luke had told him:

'You'd better wait until winter settles in if you're going to try it on foot. Without a horse, you'll just get your brains baked out walking and probably end up worse off than you are now.'

'Wait 'til winter,' Tick-Tock had said thoughtfully. 'Do we even have a winter around here? And how do I know I'll still be alive by then?'

Now, with the promise of a day off, Tick-Tock's good spirits seemed to have returned. They made their way down the slope and then turned toward the bunkhouse.

They were approaching the place wearily when the gunshots rang out. Three bullets flew past them, slapping into the walls of the bunkhouse. As they threw themselves to the hot, hard earth, the shooting continued. Someone laughed out loud with pleasure.

6

It was up to Billy Rafferty. It was his father's property, after all. From the ground he shouted angrily, 'Knock it off! There are men over here!' There was a muffled conversation, a silence. As Luke watched from the earth, Billy rose and dusted himself off, marching toward the shooters, anger visible in the set of his shoulders, the clenching of his fists. Luke rose and followed cautiously.

They found two men standing just outside the kitchen door. One had his pistol holstered, the other still held his loosely. By the lantern light from within, Luke was able to get a clear look at them. One was tall, rangy. He wore a yellow shirt and black jeans. He was the one still holding his gun. The other wore a torn red-checked shirt and faded blue denims. He was broad and nasty-looking, as if he had just come from a saloon fight and was waiting for the next one to begin. Billy did not slow his pace as he approached them.

'My name's Billy Rafferty; do you mind telling me what you're doing, unloading your pistols out here?'

'Nothing, kid,' the wide man said. 'We saw an owl perched on that fence post over there, like a target in a shooting gallery. We took it as an invitation to blow the feathers off him.'

'I hope you missed,' Billy said with emphasis.

'The light's bad,' the narrow man said. 'Earl here don't normally miss anything he shoots at. Me, I had to take my shots while the owl was on the wing.'

Which, Luke thought, was a left-handed manner of bragging. Billy was undeterred.

'This is my uncle's property. Keep those guns holstered while you're on it.'

'We should,' the narrow man agreed. 'We don't need any target practice.'

Another concealed boast, Luke thought.

These two were cocksure, long-time criminals, and he knew that Virgil Sly, Boston Sears, or both had sent for them for whatever job they had planned. The two newcomers remained in place, noting that neither Billy nor Luke was carrying a weapon. Slowly the narrow man holstered his pistol, and after a minute they turned their backs and tramped back through the kitchen. Susan could be seen hurriedly taking herself aside. Billy, Luke noticed, was trembling with the excitement.

'I've got to talk to Uncle Frank,' he said to Luke, 'but I think the matter's settled for now.' Then he too entered the house.

'I'd think so too,' Luke muttered. Though you never knew with this type of men. Luke thought that they would gun down a man as quickly as an owl. Out here who would ever know of it, or care?

He rejoined Tick-Tock and they slipped into the bunkhouse to wait for Susan to bring their supper.

She arrived fifteen minutes later, looking harried, flustered and exhausted. Luke's heart went out to the little blonde. She halted near the table, looked around and said, 'Those men!' as she dropped the tray between them. She glanced at Luke with a look that seemed to say, 'You were bad enough, but this is the limit.'

'What happened, Miss Susan?' Tick-Tock asked.

'Pawing, snide remarks. I can't walk by one of them without him grabbing at my skirt. Father tells them to stop, but it does no good. Virgil Sly and Boston don't say a word to them. I suppose the only women they've ever met are dance-hall girls.'

'Your cousin sure took an instant dislike to them,' Tick-Tock told her. 'Billy told them this was your land and they'd have to keep their guns holstered.'

'Oh, Cousin Billy means well, but what can he do, really? Half of this land belongs to Boston Sears.' She glanced at Luke again. Her expression indicated that she regarded him as useless as well.

'Well, Billy's talking to your father,' Tick-Tock said, helping himself to a slab of cornbread and a bowl of pinto beans. 'Maybe Frank can talk to Sears and put a stop to it.'

'Maybe,' Susan said, poking at her loose hair with nervous fingers. 'But aside from putting up with them, I have to serve them! I don't know what Father's talking would accomplish with Sears or Virgil Sly. Though I have noticed that Sly must have said something because they stay well out of that woman Dee Dee's way. I hate to admit it, but maybe a woman does need a protector out here. The only solution is for them to ride away, which I think will be soon from the little I've overheard.'

'Let's hope so,' Tick-Tock said around a mouthful of food. 'Lord knows you're already working too hard, Miss Susan.'

'Thanks for caring, Tick-Tock,' Susan

said with a manufactured smile. Then she swung away and was gone again, as usual having said not a word to Luke Walsh.

'I really don't think she cares for you,' Tick-Tock said to Luke.

'It doesn't seem so,' Luke answered before digging in to the food.

Billy was back before they had finished eating. There was fury written across his young face.

'Damn them,' he said, sailing his hat toward his bunk. No one had to ask whom he meant. Billy sagged on to a chair at the table. 'I talked to Uncle Frank. He told me that the men have been bothering Susan. He regrets ever having had dealings with Boston Sears. He knows they're just using the property as a hideout to gather a gang of thieves. Luke, Frank was in his room, and he was showing signs of palsy. He's never had that before. These men are driving him to his grave — which would trouble them not a bit.'

There was a desperate anger in Billy

Rafferty's words. 'I wanted to tell him about the mine, how we were progressing, but he just waved a feeble hand as if it no longer made any difference to him. Perhaps it doesn't.'

'Susan thinks they will all be departing soon,' Luke said. 'Maybe it's best if we just wait them out. What else can we do?'

'If they go,' Tick-Tock chipped in, 'there won't be nobody left to guard us. Maybe we can just leave, too.'

Billy was meditative for a moment. He put his hands over his face. 'I have nowhere to go, neither does Susan. We can't leave Frank on his own the way he is now. Do you know of some safe haven, Luke?'

Unwilling to tell them that he was on the run, with the charge of murdering a lawman hanging over his head, Luke just wagged his head heavily.

'Tick-Tock?'

'As you know I was on my way to Crater, hoping to find work, but it was nothing definite in the first place. I don't know what y'all could do over there.'

'Starve, likely,' Billy said. 'Without even a gun among us to try living off the land while we looked for a place to settle.'

Luke did not tell them that he had hopes of getting his guns back. That was a vague hope at best, based on a promise made to him by a well-known liar.

Billy had at least managed to learn the names of the two newcomers. The narrow, well-dressed man was named Dan Cummings. None of them had heard the name before. The other, thick-shouldered one was Earl Gross, known far and wide as a member of the Red Butte gang to which Virgil Sly had belonged. That knowledge gained them nothing. As each man rolled up on to his bunk for the night, Luke Walsh was thinking more and more about escape, and he would have wagered that Tick-Tock and Billy were sharing that idea.

Now, all they needed was a plan and, as he had told Dee Dee Bright, all the luck in the world.

★   ★   ★

It was hot, it was dusty, as the unpredictable wind blew harder, lifting the finer silt above the desert into the sullen sky. They were hungry and tired; it was a perfect day. It was *Sunday*. Luke was the last to rise. Judging by the sun it was an hour before noon, when the heat, even in the shade of the bunkhouse roof, brought him awake. He sat on his bunk for a long minute, rubbed his head and clambered down, facing the day with a yawn. He saw the juniper trees outside trembling in the heated morning wind, pulled on his boots and went out to find where the others had gotten to.

Luke walked around to the rear of the bunkhouse where a stone wall stretched from one end of the structure to the other. Someone had once planned a use for the area there, he thought; or maybe they had just needed to remove the stones to build the bunkhouse. In the center of the cleared area, Luke saw that a series of circles had been toed into the ground, forming a bull's-eye. At one end of the clearing Tick-Tock and Billy could be seen laughing and lagging stones into the circle.

They had found some sort of diversion, at least. Well, kids could amuse themselves for hours with such aimless games; so apparently could grown men when there was little else to do. Luke approached them, still yawning, still night-stunned.

'Can three play?' he asked.

'Any number can play,' Billy Rafferty told him. 'Pick your lag.' There was a small heap of stones behind Billy. Flat ones, round ones, oddly deformed small rocks. Luke picked up three or four and approached a line they had inscribed in the dusty soil. He didn't need to ask what the rules were, the game was so simple as to be self-explanatory — try to lag your stone as near to the middle of the circles as possible.

'What are we playing for?' Luke asked.

'I guess we don't know,' Tick-Tock answered. 'Bragging rights, I guess.'

'Give it a try, Luke. It's not much as entertainment goes, but it beats swinging a pick.'

Luke chose one of the malformed rocks, figuring the round ones would roll, the flat ones might skip, and aimed at the center of the concentric circles. As he lagged the stone he saw movement from the corner of his eye and turned to see Dan Cummings and Earl Gross seated on the rock wall beside them.

'This is what you desert rats do for fun?' Dan Cummings jeered. He still wore his bright-yellow shirt, black jeans and ox-blood boots. Earl Gross still looked as if he had dressed out of a rag-bag. 'Manly sorts, aren't they, Earl?'

'And I thought shooting at a hoot owl was a poor excuse for entertainment,' Gross answered with an unhealthy grin.

'Let the boys get on with their game,' Cummings said. He was much too smug for Luke's taste.

Tick-Tock, Billy and Luke continued the desultory game for a few minutes. Billy had removed his shirt. The taut bulk of his shoulders was obvious. When Tick-Tock went to pick up the rocks, Cummings deliberately spat tobacco juice beside him.

'That ought to count for something in the game, don't you think?' Cummings asked Earl Gross.

'It wasn't a bad shot,' Gross agreed.

From the direction of the house Luke Walsh now saw the broad-shouldered grizzly Boston Sears approaching. At his side was the slinky Virgil Sly, coatless on this morning, wearing a new white shirt, his hair parted in the middle and slicked back with water.

Boston said to Cummings, 'What's

going on here, Dan? Anything interesting?'

'No,' Cummings drawled. 'We were
just watching the kids at play.'

'Real interesting,' Earl Gross put in
sarcastically.

'You boys can't find a more manly
diversion?' Boston Sears asked, looking
at Luke, Billy and Tick-Tock.

'Such as?' Billy Rafferty asked challengingly.

'I don't know,' Boston Sears said,
removing his hat to scratch his woolly
head. 'How about a friendly little
boxing match?'

'I'd be happy to take any of you on,'
Billy Rafferty said. The well-developed
muscles of the chest and arms of the
shirtless man were plain to see, as was
his anger.

'I don't think your uncle would like
that,' Boston said, as if that were his
only consideration.

'I wouldn't mind going a few rounds
with the hayseed,' Earl Gross said,
nodding toward Tick-Tock.

'I'll do it,' Tick-Tock announced. Luke tried to talk him out of it.

'The man's a monster,' they heard him say as he took Tick-Tock by the shoulder.

'I ain't afraid,' Tick-Tock said as he removed his shirt to reveal a painfully thin body on which every rib could be counted.

'Knock it off,' Luke said to Boston Sears. 'This is only entertainment in your eyes. We need this man to work tomorrow.'

'He'll work,' Sears said with a broken-toothed smile. 'If he's able.'

Earl Gross was taking off his ragged shirt to reveal a furry body of immense bulk. Billy stepped forward to put his own hand on Tick-Tock's shoulder. 'I'll fight him, Tick-Tock, if that's what they want.'

Tick-Tock repeated stubbornly, 'I ain't afraid.'

'We know that,' Luke said, 'but it isn't the point. Let Billy do it. Or I'll take him on.'

Virgil Sly who had remained silent, had roughly sketched a boxing ring in the dirt with his boot. 'Have at it, boys,' Sly said without expression.

With a whoop from Dan Cummings, the two men met in the center of the ring. It was an obvious mismatch. Gross was a huge hairy ape, Tick-Tock a narrow, shaky whipping post. Billy tried again to take on the task himself. Though not much larger than Tick-Tock, years of swinging a pick had imbued his upper body with remarkable strength.

'That's all been decided,' Boston Sears told him, and there was nothing for Billy to do but sit on the wall beside Luke and watch what was sure to be a brutal beating, nothing more. Tick-Tock got off to a quick start in the middle of the ring, jolting Gross's head back with a stiff jab. Maybe it wouldn't be so bad, after all. But that was Tick-Tock's one good blow of the fight.

Angry now, Earl Gross moved in like

a wounded grizzly bear and draped himself over Tick-Tock, pounding away with lefts and rights. Luke could see the anguish on Tick-Tock's face. Within a minute Tick-Tock was clubbed down twice, rose twice and returned for more brutal treatment. At last Billy Rafferty could stand it no more.

'Stop it! This isn't a boxing match, it's murder!'

Billy stepped into the ring as Earl Gross backed away and Tick-Tock waved one last futile punch at him. Tick-Tock collapsed into Billy's arms. Luke had come forward to confront Boston Sears. Virgil Sly was behind him, smiling thinly.

'Don't ever do anything like that again,' Luke warned Sears.

'Listen, Walsh, I do as I like,' Boston said. 'What do you want to do? Fight me?'

'Not without a gun in my hands.'

'Well, I don't think that's going to happen, do you?' Sears asked, his lower lip protruding as he forced a smile.

'It might,' Luke said as the big man turned and walked away, the rest of the gang on his heels, laughing. Luke added under his breath, 'I hope it does.'

'Give me a hand, Luke,' Billy said. He was still propping up Tick-Tock. 'I don't think he can make it to the bunkhouse on his own.'

They helped Tick-Tock back into the bunkhouse and on to his bed. Both Luke and Billy were seething. Billy Rafferty muttered, 'Those bastards, who do they think they are?'

Luke Walsh only shook his head. He realized only then how passive he had become with the threat of arrest and a hanging sentence over his head. The knowledge brought a cowardly smell with it. He had been hiding himself away like some burrowing animal. The real Luke Walsh had not yet come to Gun Hill.

'Think he'll be all right?' Luke asked, studying the battered Tick-Tock.

'We should have stopped it,' Billy Rafferty said.

'We did all we could.'

'Not all,' Billy snapped, gently covering Tick-Tock with a light blanket although the day remained hot. That was the moment Susan chose to burst into the bunkhouse. Her face was pallid, her voice anguished.

'He's not here — I'd hoped he was,' she said somewhat incoherently.

'Who?' her cousin asked.

'Father! He's missing.'

'What do you mean, missing?' Billy asked, taking her by the shoulders.

'He's gone! He was in bed, saying something about wanting to visit the mine to see how it was coming along. I assumed he would come over here to get one of you to help him up the slope. Oh, God!' she said, collapsing on Billy's bunk, her hands covering her eyes. 'He's lost on the mountain somewhere. You know how poorly he was doing, Billy. Anything could have happened to him.'

'We'll have a look, Susan. Want to come along, Luke?'

'I'd better, I guess,' Luke Walsh answered.

Frank Rafferty hadn't made it to the mine. They found him halfway up the rugged path which led that way, curled up in the dusty soil. Billy rushed to his uncle, scrambling over the rocky ground. He examined the old man's body quickly, then turned a desolate face up to Luke. 'He's dead. What's going to become of us now?'

Together they toted the body of Frank Rafferty back down Gun Hill. Susan, who had already accepted the idea that her father was dead, nevertheless broke into uncontrollable sobbing as they appeared. She rushed toward their unhappy burden and began murmuring distant and disjointed words. Billy's face was dark, his own thoughts unspoken.

On her knees over her father's body, Susan raised her head and shouted. 'They've killed him!'

No one else said a word. When she rose, Susan told Billy, 'Bury him in a safe place, away from the animals.' Billy's answer was a slow nod. Susan looked around frantically and asked the men, 'Can I sleep in the bunkhouse tonight? I don't know what I might do if I go back to the house.'

'Sure,' Billy told her. 'Of course you can, but they'll wonder where you are at supper time.'

Susan flared up, 'Let them . . . eat owl!'

Then she began weeping again, a soft, distant, heart-breaking sound. Billy and Luke Walsh set to work.

When they had finished their unhappy task under a smoky blue sky, Billy, who had been forced to use his pick on a Sunday after all, said to Luke, 'You and Tick-Tock are right — it's time to get out of here. When the outlaws are gone we'll devise our own scheme. What we need mostly is weapons and horses.'

'There's the wagon team,' Luke suggested. Less confidently he said, 'I believe I can find us a few guns.'

7

There was no way to reach Dee Dee on that afternoon except to send Susan back to the house, and Luke would not do that. The girl's mind was made up. She would have done anything for her father, but with Frank Rafferty gone, she would do nothing at all for what she called a 'bunch of leeches'.

So, Luke figured, the outlaws would have to make their own sandwiches, Emma Sears would have to boil their coffee and Dee Dee Bright would have to rinse out her own dainties. Probably it did not matter to the gang members. Their movements made it all but certain that they would be leaving in the morning to take care of whatever business they had in mind. As for Emma Sears, no one could care much what happened to her except possibly her son.

Which brought to Luke's mind something that had to be settled and so he sat down softly beside Billy Rafferty on his bunk and told the blond kid honestly, 'We have to take Dee Dee Bright with us or the plan won't work.'

Susan, who had taken the second bunk along the opposite wall, lifted her head. She seemed about to voice an objection, but held her tongue.

'Just why is that, Luke?' Billy asked with something close to unhappiness.

'Well, for one thing,' Luke replied, 'I gave her my word.' He glanced at Susan who had turned over to face the wall. 'For another, she's the one who has my guns hidden somewhere. And I have a feeling we will need them.'

Billy was quick to remind him, 'Virgil Sly won't take it kindly if we spirit his woman away.'

'Probably not, but that's the way it has to be.' Not that he thought Sly had any deep affection for Dee Dee, at least none that was obvious, but in his eyes she was his possession, and a useful one. To take her would be an insult to his manhood. Yet, Dee Dee Bright had made it clear that she was ready to cut ties with the Red Butte gunman.

After all, she was the key to this whole business. She could tell them when the gang was leaving and hand out Luke's weapons — without which, they did not doubt, they had no chance in the wild country.

'All right, all right,' Billy said after a moment of conferring with himself, 'she goes. Tell her to come to us the minute she hears when they're pulling out.'

'I can't get in to talk to her,' Luke said. 'Sly would shoot me out of hand if he saw me around her.'

'I can do it,' a reluctant Susan said from her bunk. 'But Luke . . . are you sure you can trust that . . . woman?'

'Far from it,' he was forced to admit. 'But we have a plan now, and I suggest we stick to it.'

Susan rose heavily in a flutter of skirts and moved toward the front door, obviously unhappy about her task.

When she had slipped outside, Luke asked Billy: 'Does any of this bother you? I mean, leaving the mine and your dreams behind you, Billy?'

'The dream was my uncle's, not mine,' Billy said soberly. 'I was willing to pursue it for the man who raised me when I had no one else. Now he's gone.' Billy stretched and yawned. 'I suppose it's time for me to move along, pursue a new life. To tell you the truth, Luke,' Billy said with one of his recently infrequent smiles, 'I never thought there was more gold to be found up there than what old Clancy Gunn had already found.' He sighed. 'But we kept on digging, even though I had my doubts about the way we were going about it. Uncle Frank, you understand, had this hope ... ' His voice faded away.

'We'll have to wait and see if Susan can get a few words with Dee Dee Bright. Then we go,' Billy Rafferty said.

'Then we go,' Luke agreed. Both men

sat on Billy's bunk, looking at the bruised and beaten, huddled form of Tick-Tock, their anger and sense of urgency building.

An hour later, as the pagan sun began drifting lower across the western sky, Susan returned in a fluttering rush and said to Luke in passing, 'She'll meet you out back after sundown.'

'What did she say?' Luke had to ask Billy. His attention had not been focused on Susan, although it was now, as the girl rolled up into her bunk. It was as if Susan was unwilling to spend a moment to pass on useful information. Not to him.

'She said,' Billy answered, 'that Dee Dee will meet you outside after dark.' The kid was grinning and Luke gave him an elbow in the ribs for his attitude.

Wincing, Billy made another remark. 'I think my cousin is pretty taken with you, Luke Walsh.'

'I think you're crazy,' Luke answered, lowering his voice because of Susan's proximity. In a whisper he said, 'The way she's been giving me the silent treatment, the way she seems crazy-jealous over Dee Dee? Why would she act like that if she cared a whit about me?'

Billy lifted his eyes and said, 'And here I thought that you were a well-traveled man.'

It was still hot, but Luke went to his bunk on the second tier of the rack where it was hotter yet, next to the ceiling, and tried to both remain calm and think things out, both at once. He had always considered it best to take care of matters one item at a time. It kept things from getting scattered and confused. All right then — keep Susan out of the thoughts she inspired for now; find out more practically what Dee Dee could tell them about the Red Butte gang's plans, and discover whether or not she had recovered his weapons.

Once off Gun Hill, things would have to play out as they would.

He managed to fall asleep in the heat of the bunkhouse afternoon, only occasionally wishing that Susan Rafferty were not sleeping so near to him.

★ ★ ★

Dusk settled, fading the land to deep purple and then the sky darkened. Luke had no idea what time Dee Dee would be able to slip out of the house, so he rose and went out the door to wait for her. No matter how long it took, he needed to talk to the woman. There would be no better chance for all of them, for Luke, for Susan, Billy or poor Tick-Tock. And no better chance for Dee Dee if she was sincere about leaving the outlaw, Virgil Sly.

The half-moon had risen, a lazy, slowly opening eye above the peaks beyond, and Dee Dee Bright appeared like a moth fluttering before its light. 'Well?' she asked, breathlessly rushing into his arms.

Luke, despite all good intentions, did nothing to push the woman away. She was alive, vibrant, and all female. They had spent many happy moments in her bed. He could never forget them. Nor could he fail to realize that those days were gone; their relationship had to change. He accepted her kisses for a minute, then stepped back.

'Let's stick to business,' he said in a way which seemed to puzzle Dee Dee. Luke saw her frown, saw her eyes narrow in the moonlight.

'It's the little blonde, isn't it? Susan?' Dee Dee asked.

He thought he might as well admit it. 'Yes.'

'All right,' Dee Dee said with a puff of air. 'I can understand that.' She paused before she asked, 'You're still taking me away, aren't you?'

'If you still want to go. Did you find the guns?'

'Yes. I hid them away in the pantry behind some sacks of flour and beans.'

'Terrific. All we need to know now is

when Virgil and the gang are pulling out of here.'

'In the morning, before dawn from what I overheard. But it will still be risky, won't it?'

'It will be risky. When you're sure they're gone, come over to the bunkhouse. Susan is already there,' he told her. Dee Dee squinted inquiringly at him in the darkness.

'It's nothing like that,' he felt compelled to say. 'Billy and Tick-Tock are going with us.'

'So many?'

'Yes, we're taking the freight wagon.'

'What about Emma Sears — she'll raise hell.'

'It doesn't matter, there'll be no one to hear her. Let her stand and scream at the mountain.'

'And suck eggs,' Dee Dee said with a faint smile.

'If she can find any.'

'All right, we'll do it your way,' Dee Dee agreed. 'I need to get back to civilization somehow. This place . . .'

She patted at her hair and smoothed her silk skirt.

'I know,' Luke told her. 'I feel the same way.'

'Luke?' Dee Dee asked a little coyly, 'do you mind if I kiss you one last time.'

How do you answer that? Luke shook his head and let her rise to tiptoes to deliver one of her familiar, warm kisses, her arms looped around his waist.

'Just so you'll remember what you'll be missing,' she said. She then slipped something cold and solid into his hand. 'Partial payment,' Dee Dee said with a wide smile. Luke didn't have to glance down. The feel of his Colt .44 was quite familiar to him.

'Loaded?' he asked.

'I imagine. I don't go around unloading guns,' Dee Dee answered. 'I would have got your belt and holster, but I couldn't figure out how to conceal them.' She gave him a quick peck on the cheek and said, 'Till tomorrow, then.' She scurried away through the darkness.

Luke started back to the bunk-house, shoving the pistol behind his belt. He had thought he had been left alone in the darkness, but he was wrong. He saw Susan's slender figure appear, hurrying away from him. What had she seen; what had she imagined?

One thing was certain: he was not making a good impression on the pretty little girl.

Returning to the barracks himself, he saw Susan on her bunk, saw Tick-Tock looking pale and sick, lying on his bed. Billy was sitting up on his bed, interested. Luke lifted his shirt to reveal the Colt revolver he was now carrying.

'Dee Dee says they're thinking of pulling out before dawn tomorrow. I told her to come over here after they go. She'll be bringing my Winchester along with her.'

'It's still going to be rough,' Billy said, glancing in the direction of Susan and Tick-Tock.

'Two of us against four armed men . . . '

'I don't think they care if we go; why would they?'

'There's Dee Dee,' Billy pointed out. 'Virgil Sly might not like finding her gone.'

'That's true,' Luke admitted. 'The bigger problem is the desert itself. We need to haul all of the water we can collect.' Billy's face was still not encouraging. Luke had to tell him, 'I'm going, Billy, that's it! And I have to take Tick-Tock and Dee Dee with me. They want to leave. You and your cousin,' he glanced again at Susan who could not possibly be asleep, but was pretending to be, 'have to decide for yourselves. This is — was your home, after all. As for me — I'm gone with the first light of day if everything works out. With or without you.'

He turned sharply toward his bunk. Billy lifted a hand and touched Luke's elbow. Softly he said:

'We're going with you. What's left for us here?'

★　★　★

Luke awoke just after dawn. A mosquito of which they had few, probably due to the lack of nearby water, had bitten him on the ear. It was either that which had brought him out of his sleep or the persistent pecking sound, such as a small bird might make, coming from the front door. Glancing that way he saw the figure of Dee Dee Bright in a fur-trimmed hooded cape, and he came suddenly alert, realizing what prompted her pre-dawn appearance.

Luke swung down and tramped toward the door, scratching his ear as a blue eye peered up at him. Susan, it seemed, had not slept soundly.

'Is it on?' he hissed over-loudly at Dee Dee.

'They're gone — half an hour ago. I don't know how long you want to wait,' she whispered in return.

135

'Just long enough to make sure they haven't decided to return. Can you keep watch from the front of the house?'

Dee Dee nodded silently and walked that way. Luke went to Billy's bunk and shook his shoulder to rouse him.

'What is it?' Billy Rafferty asked sleepily.

'We're ready to move out — if you're still going with us.'

'I'm going. Hand me my boots and I'm ready.'

'What about Tick-Tock?'

'We'll let him sleep as long as possible, then we'll have to carry him out. I'll get the wagon team hitched. You can wake Susan.'

'I'm awake,' she said testily, as if she didn't want Luke around her bunk.

'Good,' Billy said. 'Want to help me with the harness, then?'

She sat up and nodded. She was still dressed in a chemise, and briefly she crossed her arms in front of her. 'If I can have a minute to dress.'

'You're the one who wanted to sleep with the boys,' Billy gibed.

'I'll help you with the hitching,' Luke said, 'though I haven't handled harnesses for some time.'

'They haven't changed any,' said Billy Rafferty, who was in an unusually playful mood on this dark morning. 'Then we start collecting water, right? All we can find.'

'I'd say so. It's a plan. Dee Dee is watching to see that nothing brings the gang back this way.'

'All right, that's good, too,' Billy said.

'Dee Dee Bright is an all-around useful woman,' they heard Susan say sharply. She was holding her blue-checked gingham dress in front of her, waving them out of the bunkhouse.

Billy said in a low voice, 'I see you still haven't gotten that business straightened out with my cousin.'

'I'm not sure I ever will,' Luke answered as they stepped outside. 'It's hard to have a conversation with someone who refuses to listen.' He didn't muffle his voice, and he glanced back at Susan who must have heard his response. Her face reddened as if she were trying to come up with some cutting retort, but in the end she said nothing as the two men strode away toward the barn where the team of horses stood waiting.

Billy paused briefly, looking away toward where his uncle lay buried. Luke asked him:

'What are you thinking? Wishing we could take him with us?'

Billy shook his head. 'No, he belongs up here. It consumed a large portion of his life — and mine and Susan's as well. I wish he could have found his gold, but I can't see how it would really have made any difference in the end, anyway.'

'He's not the first man to use up his life chasing a dream,' Luke said, 'and he certainly won't be the last. You were always loyal to him; that's something to remember.'

'Yeah, I guess,' Billy said. His mood

changing, he swung open the barn doors and stalked to the two eager-looking gray horses standing in the shadows. 'They look fresh enough, don't you think? We'll take them outside and then back them up to the wagon before we start fooling with the harness.'

'You're the boss on this job, Billy; I'm sure you know best.'

Dee Dee had returned to watch them silently as they finished buckling the team down. 'Virgil and the boys are miles away,' she said in a slightly fearful voice. She was holding Luke's Winchester and his belt holster. Now she handed them to him. 'I couldn't find any more weapons hidden in the house.' She glanced at Billy, who shook his head.

'There must be a couple of weapons in there, but I don't know where they'd be. I don't think we have the time to tear the place apart, searching.' He paused as he had a second thought. Tightening the throat latch on the off-wheel gray horse he asked Dee Dee, 'What about the old woman?'

'Emma? She was still asleep the last time I saw her — probably waiting for Susan to serve her breakfast in bed.'

'Those days are gone,' Billy said with a small flare-up of temper. 'Let the old goose drag herself out of bed and fix herself something to eat.'

'What about you, Dee Dee?' Luke asked. 'Is there anything you need to take?' He was settling his Colt back into its familiar holster.

'I have the one trunk I brought with me, which I've finished packing — if it's not too much trouble.'

'It's a small enough repayment,' Luke said. On the bunkhouse step he saw Susan watching them, a small pout on her lips. 'How about you, Susan?' Luke asked in a louder voice, 'is there anything you need to pack and take with you from the house?'

'Nothing could persuade me to go back into that place,' she said firmly. 'I'll gather up all the canteens I can find and start filling them.'

'I thought you and she . . . ' Dee Dee said, poking Luke's arm.

'That's true. She just doesn't know it yet.'

'Is it because of me?' Dee Dee asked, her eyes showing genuine concern.

'What do you think?' Luke asked tautly.

'I think we'd better get my trunk out of the house,' she replied.

It was just past seven in the morning when they were ready to roll the wagon out of there. They had taken Tick-Tock to the wagon and placed him on a bed made with his own cot's mattress and a few blankets. They had to support him, but he moved under his own power enough, so that they didn't actually carry him. He was battered up still from Earl Gross's beating, but seemed to be making a recovery.

On the way to the heavy wagon he had asked, 'Are we leaving now?' and when Luke told him that they were, Tick-Tock had winked at them and said. 'Good. I was getting a little tired of this place, boys.'

They placed him as gently as possible into the wagon bed and set a canteen near him in case he should get thirsty. Luke looked down at the man, knowing just how he felt. It had been a long trip into Gun Hill; it would be a long trip out.

Luke had to go back into the house to help Dee Dee with her blue trunk. He and Billy hefted it into the back of the wagon. For an item which was presumably filled only with a woman's frilly gew-gaws, it was surprisingly heavy.

They waited for Susan, who came back carrying only a flour sack filled with a few sandwiches.

'Going on a picnic, are we, Cousin?' Billy said, taking a place on the bench seat and gathering up the reins. 'Well, then, let's have at it.'

Luke sat next to Billy with his rifle upright between his legs. Susan and Dee Dee had been helped up on to the flatbed, where they sat as far away from each other as possible. Billy kicked off the brake and started the gray horses down the long grade leading to open desert.

About fifty yards from the house a shrill screaming came to them. They turned to see Emma Sears, her steel-gray hair in a tangle, standing on the porch yelling after them. No one bothered to respond. They had the long road ahead to think about. That and the four gunmen who would be out on the desert somewhere ahead. Billy guided the team of horses uncertainly onward.

8

Luke Walsh had nearly forgotten how brutally hot the desert could become at midday. On the playa flats they caught none of the occasional breeze that teased them on Gun Hill. The heavy wheels of the freight wagon cut long, shallow parallel lines into the playa; the white, flat land was a blistering furnace, branding Luke Walsh's back as he leaned forward on the wagon seat, looking vainly for respite.

Five or six buzzards hovered against the pale blue sky above them. They seemed to unnerve Tick-Tock. Dee Dee placed some sort of sheer veil over the injured man's eyes to shield them from sun glare and to obscure his view of the devil birds. The wagon rolled on across endless miles of naked desert.

'Well,' Billy said, wiping his brow. 'I haven't seen a sign of them.' The illusory image of a lake gleamed in front of them, always retreating as they drew nearer. Men had died pursuing mirages they believed to be water out here.

'Neither have I,' Luke said, 'nor of anyone else. Where are you taking us, Billy?'

'Tucson's the only place that makes sense to me,' Billy Rafferty told him. 'Unless you've got a better idea.'

'No, no I don't,' Luke replied. Though Tucson was the last place he wanted to go. They were undoubtedly still looking for the man who had killed Marshal Stoddard there. It was risky to go anywhere near the town. He couldn't think of another suggestion. Luke didn't know the territory well enough to offer a different plan.

Seeing the uneasiness in Luke's eyes, Dee Dee tried to help. Placing her forearms up on the back rest of the wagon seat, she said, 'That's right where Virgil and the rest of the gang will be heading. I think they're after the bank. For another thing, Virgil — and Boston Sears, too — are determined to kill that little rat, Cotton Werth for turning on the Red Butte gang.'

'I hadn't considered that,' Luke said. He asked Billy hopefully, 'What do you think? We could run right into them on the street.'

'I'd like to run into Boston Sears,' Billy said with dark anger. 'But you could be right; it may not be the best of ideas.'

'There's Crater,' Tick-Tock muttered from under the blue veil Dee Dee had placed on his face.

'How far's that?' Billy asked.

'About the same as Tucson. I'd say twenty miles, except it's to the north.' They knew that Crater was where Tick-Tock had been headed when he started on his desert journey.

'What's there?' Dee Dee asked.

'Little enough. There's the crater, of course. They have a couple of hotels, a stable and a stage line through twice a week.'

Billy looked apprehensively north-ward where a low line of saw-toothed hills could be seen. 'I don't know.' He shook his head. 'Do you know the way, Tick-Tock?'

'Thought I did. The man who wrote and told me about a job up there drew a map for me. I lost that with my mule, but sure, we can find it easy enough.'

'What's your thinking, Luke?' Billy asked.

'Why not give it a try? I really don't think we want to run into the Red Butte boys in Tucson. Besides, if there's a stage line we can always travel on from there.'

'On what money?' Billy asked.

'Well, if you planned to go on by stage, you wouldn't need this team and wagon any longer. They could be sold and you could buy a ticket to anywhere you want to go.'

'I'm not sure there is any place I want to go,' Billy said looking now more haggard and beaten down than Luke had ever seen him. He asked

Susan across his shoulder just as the wagon hit a jarring bump, 'What about you, cousin? Any place you'd like to go?'

'I have an aunt in Las Flores — a great-aunt, actually — but I don't know if I'd want to go and live there.'

'There's time to figure that out later,' Billy said as he slowly turned the team northward. 'I think we should get as far away from the Red Butte gang as possible.'

'You haven't said anything, Dee Dee,' Luke commented, turning his head toward the dark-haired girl on the wagon bed.

'What do I care? It's all the same to me, but I agree that we have to get away from Virgil Sly and that bunch of killers. Anywhere where Virgil can't find me is all right with me.'

'I suppose you can find work most anywhere,' Susan said to Dee Dee, and it was not a friendly remark.

'Probably,' Dee Dee replied softly. 'But I'm thinking of retiring and settling down.' She gave Luke a long steady look and a smile which he knew was fabricated only to annoy Susan. Susan Rafferty leaned back against the side of the wagon bed, folding her arms and scowling out at the desert emptiness. Billy was feeling playful. Without turning his head he said, 'That's a good idea, Dee Dee. Maybe you and Susan could find a little house and move in together.'

Luke nudged Billy, but it didn't keep Billy Rafferty from breaking out into a huge grin which he wore for the next mile.

★ ★ ★

Not long after that Billy felt the horses faltering slightly with the heat and the long miles. Slowly he drew them up. 'We've got to rest and water the team, folks. It wouldn't do to have them go down out here. Did someone remember to get a bucket?'

Susan said, 'I brought two, along

with extra canteens and the water bags.'

'You're a good girl,' Billy said lightly. She shot back, 'And you are a dirty skunk!' Billy just smiled again, and after a moment, Susan smiled back. It was the same beautiful smile Luke remembered but had not seen for days.

Billy set the brake and they all clambered down as the horses were given water. 'We'll give them an hour,' Billy said. Shading his eyes, he looked at the hills ahead. 'I hope we can find a pass through those.'

'There's got to be one,' Luke said.

'Do you know where the pass is, Tick-Tock?'

'Not exactly,' Tick-Tock said from the wagon bed. He lifted an arm that pointed nowhere and muttered, 'Up ahead.'

'With any luck we'll cut someone's sign,' Luke said. 'Someone who knows where he's going.'

Dee Dee was standing near them, dabbing at her face and throat with a damp handkerchief. 'It's so hot!' she said. 'If we find this town I am going to buy all the ice I can find and take a bath in it.'

'That's a disgusting image,' Susan said.

'That's because you're the wrong sex,' Billy laughed. Luke stayed out of the by-play, but he himself found the unlikely scene intriguing. He tried to erase the image from his mind. He stood looking instead at Susan's narrow back, at the gentle flare of her hips, at the blond tendrils of hair drifting in the barely stirring breeze. There had to be a way to break through her dislike of him, her concept of him as some sort of rough country roué.

Patience, he counseled himself, was the only solution. There would come a time when she would realize that he was right for her.

Billy was tossing the buckets back into the wagon. The horses stood patiently beneath the white sun. 'Hop in, ladies,' he said. 'We may as well try to make a few more miles today.'

With everyone aboard again, Billy started the horses forward once more, plodding toward the smoky hills. Luke squinted into the sun, looking in either direction at the ground they passed over, searching for some clue as to where better-informed travelers had gone before them. They might find themselves regretting this decision by nightfall, finding themselves only more distant from Tucson. Billy shared his qualms, and they rode on silently as the dying sun coasted toward the far western horizon.

In the wagon bed their three sun-beaten passengers were also silent. Tick-Tock wasn't up to conversation, and Susan and Dee Dee had no interest in talking to each other. The miles passed with incredible slowness beneath the hoofs of the gray horses.

Luke's hand suddenly shot up. 'Hold up, Billy. I've caught some sign.'

'Another wagon?'

'I don't think many wagons come this way, do you? No, but there were two

152

men riding this way, and not long ago. I think we should follow them along. Their tracks are veering a little eastward. What do you think?'

'I don't think we have much choice,' Billy said, again mopping his face with his bandanna. 'There's only a couple of hours of daylight left, and we've got to find that pass or give it up and head back toward Tucson.'

'That's the way it seems to me.' Luke turned his head toward the bed of the wagon. 'Is Tick-Tock doing any better? He might have some idea of where we are.'

'He's just the same,' Dee Dee answered. 'You won't get much help from him.'

Trustingly, they started the team and began following the tracks of the strange riders. It seemed to be their only choice. Luke was still dreading returning to Tucson for any reason. Most towns did not take kindly to having their marshal gunned down.

The ground began to soften as they

neared the looming hills. Billy told them. 'I can make out the tracks plainly now.'

Luke only nodded. He was only happy to be off the long extent of playa, even though they did not know where they were going. Billy raised an arm and a smile creased his face. Abruptly ahead of them a gap in the hills had appeared, and they thought they could see a narrow trail leading up to the crest. That was the direction in which the unknown horsemen had headed.

'I think we've found it,' Billy said cheerfully.

'I hope so — it seems it must be the way, doesn't it?'

Billy halted the team again at the foot of the trail leading up on to the naked hills. Luke swung down and entered the gap where he was able to clearly make out the tracks of two ridden horses traveling upward.

When he came back, he said, 'Well, we know it can be ridden, but do you think the wagon can make it?'

Billy nodded. 'It's steep, all right, and the horses are pretty beat up, but I think we can do it.' He grinned. 'Besides, there's really no choice, is there? We'll water the horses again and let them have a little rest, then we'll give it a try.'

Luke nodded, then said, 'If you ladies want to step down, you have a few minutes.'

Dee Dee slid rapidly off the wagon's tailgate, and with hoisted skirts, headed for a nearby stand of creosote brush. Susan's mouth formed a disparaging moue and she slipped slowly to the ground, dragging the two zinc buckets with her as Luke retrieved a canvas water bag from the back of the wagon.

While the horses drank their fill Luke and Billy went ahead fifty yards or so, surveying the rugged trail. They could see a quarter of a mile or so up ahead, then the road curved away out of view.

Looking up, Billy said, 'We can make it that far at least. If the trail doesn't narrow drastically around the bend we should be all right.'

'I wonder how far Crater actually is,' Luke said.

'No telling, but my guess would be over the ridge and down the far side. We should be able to spot any town from the crest line. If we can't do it today, we'll make it tomorrow.'

'Even if we have to walk?'

'I won't kill the horses,' Billy Rafferty said with determination. 'We'll have to hope there's some sort of park or just a patch of flat ground where we can hold them overnight if it comes to that.'

'You're right. They're about your only asset right now, aren't they.'

'Just about,' Billy agreed, his expression grim.

Shadows were already settling within the gap as the sun lowered. 'If we're going to move on tonight, we'd better get going,' Luke commented.

'You're right.' Billy looked up the rugged slope again and muttered, 'I wouldn't want to try that trail after dark.'

With the purple ghosts of sundown haunting the canyons, they started up the long, treacherous trail into the unknown hills. Billy hunched far forward as he guided the horses carefully upward. Looking down from his side of the box, Luke could see that the wheels of the wagon were only inches from the gorge on their right. He found himself clenching his rifle tightly, as if that were doing him any good.

When they reached the point in the trail where it curved away eastward, the traveling became surprisingly easier. The grade was not so steep and the trail widened enough to actually be termed a road. Billy leaned back and his grip on the reins lightened. He glanced at Luke.

'I wouldn't want to do that every day,' Luke commented.

'I wouldn't want to do it ever again,' Billy answered. 'Let's hope the road going down is good.'

'You're sure the road will crest out?'

'Luke, sane people don't build roads that go nowhere.'

Both men were more relaxed now. From time to time they passed more stunted juniper trees like those that grew on Gun Hill: wind-sheared, dusty and dry. Luke glanced toward the bed of the wagon. The women were pale and obviously wearied by the tension of the ascent. Dee Dee winked broadly at him. Whether Susan saw it or not he could not tell. Dee Dee seemed to have grown fond of needling the blonde girl. Luke turned his attention back to the darkening trail.

'I hope we can find a place to pull over, Billy. This isn't going to be any good, traveling an unknown trail after dark.'

'No, it's not. If we can't find a spot, we'll just have to pull up and figure on us all spending the night on the wagon bed.'

But luck, or the most they had had of it for a while, was with them. Because as they followed the road into a slight declivity, they came upon a tiny park where a dozen or so scrub oak trees grew.

'Here's our place!' Billy said happily.

Luke answered soberly, 'It looks like we may have to share it.' He shifted the Winchester so that it rested across his lap and gestured toward two horses standing tethered in the pooled shadows of the oaks.

'The riders we followed up here,' Billy said.

'That's right,' Luke said. Billy slowed the team, then drew it to a halt.

'What do you think?' Billy asked in a taut whisper.

'I don't know. They could be honest travelers or . . . I don't know. Here,' Luke said, shoving the Winchester into Billy's hands.

Luke slipped from the wagon seat and moved forward through the shadows cast by the trees, Colt revolver in his hand.

He could see no men about, but he caught the faint scent of wood smoke; a small fire was burning somewhere. Nearing the horses, he saw that they were flaked with froth and unsteady on their feet; both looked near to foundering. These men had ridden hard and apparently cared little about their ponies.

Luke was reluctant to go on farther, but there wasn't much choice. It was that or leave the women and Tick-Tock to sleep in the wagon on the edge of the dangerous trail, and who was to say that these men, whoever they were, would not come there out of curiosity? He turned and started back to where the others waited, not knowing what decision to make.

He nearly walked into the stranger in the darkness. But it was no stranger. He recognized the man by the faint glow of the rising moon. And by the yellow shirt he wore. It was the dandified, lean gunman, Dan Cummings.

'You might as well drop that gun, Walsh,' Cummings said. 'I've got you in my sights.'

That was the last thing Luke Walsh intended to do. He fired wildly and rolled to one side as Cummings's gun exploded, darting flame past his head. Coming up on to one knee Luke took more careful aim and shot the wounded, staggering outlaw once more. The man's legs buckled and his pistol slid to the ground from his limp fingers. Luke rushed toward him.

Turning Cummings on to his back he saw that the man was still alive, but barely. Cummings's eyes studied Luke. He seemed to nod slightly. 'I underestimated you,' Cummings said hoarsely 'I never thought you'd be that good.'

'Why'd you want to shoot me?' Luke asked, crouching down beside Cummings. A trickle of blood now leaked from the corner of the badman's mouth and ran unheeded down his cheek.

'It wasn't personal,' Cummings said, coughing heavily. 'We saw you coming up the trail and wanted your horses. You've seen our mounts — we ran them into the ground. Held up the Tucson

161

bank and got away clean. We split up . . . ' There were now long intervals between Dan Cummings's words. 'Sly and Boston Sears decided that . . . they had to take care of the rat, Cotton Werth before they left town . . . me and Earl Gross just wanted to hit the trail, fast. To hell with Cotton Werth.'

'Who has the bank money?' Luke asked.

'Looking to get your hands on it?' Cummings asked, his eyes gleaming in the moonlight.

'No.'

'Virgil Sly has it. We were all going to meet at Crater and split the loot after they finished their own business. Looks like we're not going to . . . '

That was all he said. Luke checked the man's pulse, and that made it definite. Dan Cummings was dead. It was probably just as well, there was nothing they or anyone could have done for Cummings after the lead he had taken.

Shaking his head, Luke rose to his

feet and started back through the moon shadows of the oak grove to where the wagon stood. Billy Rafferty, the Winchester at his feet, stood beside the freight wagon with his hands flung high. Tick-Tock wobbled against the bed near by and Earl Gross, his gun steady in his hand, was leering at Dee Dee and Susan.

9

'Just stand steady, Rafferty,' Earl Gross was saying. 'We don't want you — just the horses. And maybe,' he added nastily, 'the two women. We'll wait for Dan Cummings to get here and then we'll decide about that.'

'What makes you so sure that Cummings is going to get here?' Dee Dee asked challengingly. There was no quaver in her voice. She had spent much of her life bracing tough men. 'We all heard those shots. It sounded like someone was fighting back.'

'I'd put my money on Dan any time,' Gross said.

'You'd lose,' Luke said softly. He had taken a few quiet steps nearer while Earl Gross was talking.

Gross was determined to fight it out. No doubt he had visions of the life ahead of him, his pockets filled with gold from the bank job. He wasn't going to be taken. The big, ragged man spun and fired off a shot that came too near to Luke's skull, but it was a miss all the same. Luke's answering shot was not.

The bullet from his .44 caught Gross in the throat and he spun away, horror in his eyes, to clutch at his neck as blood spurted from the wound, staining his torn shirt front, covering his hands. He looked again at Luke Walsh, his eyes wide, and keeled over to die against the rough earth of the mountain road.

'How . . . ' Dee Dee asked a little breathlessly, 'did those two get here ahead of us?'

'Riding hard,' Luke answered, holstering his pistol. 'The slowest saddle mount will make good time against any wagon. And I can promise you they were riding hard. Almost killed their horses.'

'What about Virgil Sly?' Dee Dee wanted to know. Luke shook his head.

'Cummings told me that he and

Boston Sears stayed back in Tucson to hunt down the informer, Cotton Werth.'

Dee Dee only nodded. She remembered Cotton Werth well enough and the plot to hand Sly over to Marshal Stoddard. And Dee Dee knew Sly well enough to know that he would view tracking down Werth being as important as whatever money they had taken from the Tucson bank. In a way, Werth had been the one who had started all of this with his treachery. The Red Butte boys did not take disloyalty to the gang lightly.

'What do we do now?' Susan asked. She was not as fearful as Luke would have imagined she'd be. The sight of the dead man had not rattled her. Then he recalled that Boston Sears had been staying with her family and a few men who had tried to escape from Gun Hill before had been killed. Probably by Sears. He had not seen her cry since her father had died.

'We stay here for the night and press

on to Crater tomorrow,' Billy said with determination.

'That's where Sears and Virgil Sly are riding once they've finished with Werth,' Luke Walsh told him.

'It doesn't matter,' Billy Rafferty said wearily. 'The plan was to get to Crater, and that's where we have to go now. There will be a lot of people around us, and maybe some of us — those who choose to go — will be off on the stagecoach before Sly and Sears have finished their business in Tucson and ridden up here.'

'I'm taking the first stage out,' Dee Dee said. 'I'm not going to deal with Virgil Sly.'

'He's rich again,' Luke pointed out.

'Nobody's that rich,' she said firmly.

Luke nodded his agreement. 'What do you suggest we do with him, Billy?' Luke Walsh asked, indicating the body of Earl Gross.

'We've got no tools to bury him, and I haven't the inclination to do it.' Billy glanced to his right. 'We roll him off into the ravine. Let the wild things have him. He was one of their kind.'

Luke nodded, not liking the idea but realizing there was no other way. He wondered idly if someone would dispose of him so uncaringly one day.

They took Earl Gross under each arm and dragged him to the edge of the dark road. Then they rolled him off to flop and bounce and roll into the depths of the canyon. They could watch his descent by the light of the pale moon — a marionette with his strings clipped, a thing that once was a man walking the earth. He disappeared into the deep shadows of the gorge, and Luke felt himself tremble just a little. He had despised the man, but death always touches you in some way.

'Might as well go get the other one,' Luke said. 'Then we can set up a rough camp for the night.'

Tramping down the leaf-littered slope toward the oak grove, they found Cummings and dragged him back up the incline to the road where they rolled him off to join his partner in the darkness of the dead.

Dee Dee and Susan stood near each other, watching in silence, Dee Dee with her arms firmly folded.

'When are we going to eat?' The voice was Tick-Tock's and it startled all of them. It was as if he had risen from his own grave. 'I sure am hungry.'

Luke laughed and clapped the man on the shoulder. 'I'm glad you decided to rejoin us,' Luke said.

'Well, I'm glad too, but I would be happier if I knew where I was — and when we were going to eat.'

'Why don't you pull the wagon off the road, Billy?' Luke suggested. 'I'll help you with the unhitching later. Maybe if we give the other horses a little water they'll have a chance at survival, too. There's a small campfire that was burning somewhere, though I never saw it. Maybe you can track it by scent. The night might get cold this high up, and besides, we'll need to make something to eat.'

'Sandwiches and coffee,' Susan said, pulling a burlap bag from the bed of the wagon. 'That's what you're getting, and you ought to be grateful to me for packing it.'

★ ★ ★

Two hours later they were gathered around the low-burning campfire, their stomachs full, sipping at strong, bitter coffee. The wagon team had been unharnessed and picketed out. Luke had examined the ponies that Cummings and Gross had ridden. One of them, a stubby little buckskin looked as if he might recover. The other horse, a red roan, had taken a few drinks of water and then flopped down on its side — not a good sign. There was little else to be done for them; the matter would be resolved by morning one way or the other.

'I suppose we ought to sit up in shifts to watch the road,' Billy said. 'We don't need any more surprise guests tonight.'

'I'll take the first watch,' Tick-Tock volunteered. 'Lord knows I have had more than enough sleep the last twenty-four hours.'

'If you're up to it,' Billy agreed. 'I know I could use some rest right now.' He stretched his shoulders, aching from the handling of the team's reins all day.

'Don't worry about me,' Tick-Tock said. 'My shooting eye ain't tired.'

'All right — find your spot, then wake me up for the second watch. Luke can take the dawn shift.'

Luke started to object, feeling that Billy probably needed sleep more than he did, but he still habitually thought of Billy Rafferty as the job foreman, and whatever he said was fine with Luke, so long as everybody took his turn.

As Tick-Tock picked up the Winchester rifle and headed off to find a good spot from which to watch the road, Luke rolled up in a blanket he had found among the outlaws' gear and curled up to sleep, careful to position himself so that he was not too near to either Susan or Dee Dee. Yawning once, he studied the starry sky and high-floating moon for a minute, then fell off to sleep with the breeze whispering through the oaks and the near comfort of women breathing in their peaceful sleep beside him.

In the hour before dawn, Billy Rafferty shook him awake. The moon had gone down and the night had grown cold. Brittle silver stars were clustered overhead.

'There's coffee on the fire if you want to take a cup along,' Billy whispered so as not to wake the others. 'You've got the short shift, Luke. As soon as there's any light in the sky, I mean to hitch the team and get off this mountain.' He handed Luke the Winchester.

'Good idea,' Luke said, sitting up, rubbing at his tired eyes. He asked, 'Did you take a look at the two saddle ponies?'

'Haven't had a chance yet. They're the least of our worries. For now I mean to catch a couple more hours' sleep. The perch Tick-Tock found is a square boulder just past that twin oak over there.'

Luke rose heavily to his feet. He poured himself a tin cup of coffee, snatched up his blanket which he wrapped around his shoulders against the chill of the night and strode off toward the lookout point. Scooting up on to the square boulder, Luke drew the blanket more tightly around him, sipped at the coffee and watched the long trail for any sign of approaching men.

His thoughts wandered far and wide as he sat there, remembering the good times back on the Havasu Ranch, the bad days on Gun Hill and a hundred other small episodes in his so far unproductive life. But always his mind returned to Susan Rafferty. Was there any way to capture the little blonde girl's heart? If it could be done was it even fair to her? He had little to offer. His possessions now totaled one Winchester rifle, one Colt revolver — a hell of a man to pretend he had much to bring to Susan who did deserve a decent life, better than what she had had on Gun Hill.

Luke yawned again. Studying the trail below him he now believed he could make out its contours better. Glancing across his shoulder he saw pre-dawn gray creeping into the sky along the horizon. Then he heard the chinking sounds of trace chains being attached. It was nearly dawn and Billy was up and at it.

It was time to strike out for Crater once more.

Billy looked up from his work as Luke entered the camp. There was a tinge of pink in the eastern sky already. 'Everything all right?' he asked Luke.

'You didn't hear any shooting, did you?' Luke replied. 'Any coffee on?'

'Susan's boiling a new pot. It should be almost ready.'

'You two are both early risers, aren't you?'

Billy shrugged, rising from the

crouch he had been in, attaching the traces to the cross tree on the wagon. 'You know how it is on the desert, Luke. You start to work early, before the heat builds. My cousin and I have gotten used to it. I don't think either of us can sleep after dawn.'

Luke could smell fresh coffee now, but he took a moment to detour by the horses Dan Cunningham and Earl Gross had used so roughly. The buckskin's eyes were bright and it watched Luke's approach eagerly. The red roan hung its head, but at least it was on its feet. They would starve to death if left on the barren mountain, so Luke made his decision.

'I want to take those ponies along with us, Billy. They won't slow us down.'

'Do you think they can make it?'

'If they can't, we've done our best for them. I'll get Tick-Tock to help me throw their saddles and bridles in the wagon and tie the horses on a lead. How are we fixed for water? They may need another bucketful.'

'I think we've got plenty. Ask Susan — she's the one who's been in charge of the water.'

Luke was eager to talk to Susan, though he remained a little anxious. He was starting to feel less than manly. That little speck of a woman had him cowed! He strode confidently into the camp, or he hoped he appeared so, and walked up to Susan, crouched over the fire.

'I'm going to take those two outlaw horses along with us. Billy said to ask you if there's enough water so that they can drink their fill before we start.'

'Of course,' she said, looking at him, her face serene. 'We have plenty and if the poor animals need it, certainly they may have it.'

'Thanks,' was all he managed to say by way of response.

What had happened! She was actually smiling, her blue eyes sparkling with the firelight.

She lifted the heavy blue pot and

filled Luke's tin cup. He turned away, frowning in puzzlement. Tick-Tock was rising from his bed, rolling his blanket and Luke told him what they were going to do.

'Sure, Luke,' Tick-Tock said cheerfully. 'Matter of fact, I can take care of all of that for you. You just sit down and finish your coffee.'

'Thanks, Tick-Tock.'

Tick-Tock smoothed back his straw-colored hair and walked off toward where the outlaws' horses stood. Not far away from Luke, as he was rolling his own blanket, Dee Dee sat up in bed, yawning. Her blanket fell away as she stretched her arms.

'My God,' said Dee Dee, who was a habitual late-riser, 'do people actually do this every day? Get up with the roosters?'

'Afraid they do,' Luke said with a smile.

'I'm getting back to town life as soon as possible,' she said, yawning again. 'How can these people do it?'

'They probably go to bed before midnight,' Luke answered. Dee Dee laughed softly and coughed.

'I suppose they do,' she agreed. 'Who were those crazy men who first thought of inventing a clock!'

Luke sat on his blanket roll, watching Susan around the fire. He said to Dee Dee, 'I can't figure it out — she actually seems to like me again this morning. What did I do right?'

'Oh *that!*' Dee Dee waved a hand in the air. 'You didn't do anything. Last night while you were gone we had a little womanly heart to heart talk. I told her that you and I had been friends back in Tucson, but that you had always acted like a perfect gentleman with me.'

'Why, you little liar,' Luke said with a smile. Dee Dee laughed.

'Am I not? But if it made Susan happy and helps to make you happy, why not?'

'Thanks, Dee Dee.'

She gestured for his coffee cup and took a drink from it. 'Are we even now,

Luke?' Dee Dee asked.

'Not exactly,' Luke answered, 'but I just entered a large credit on your account.'

Billy was leading the team of gray horses and the wagon forward. The red roan and the buckskin horse were tethered behind. It was time to hit the road again. Crater lay just beyond the hills and they meant to be there on this day.

If their luck held. There were still a couple of angry men with guns out there. Virgil Sly, who would be angry at having Dee Dee stolen away from him, and Boston Sears, who needed no reason at all to start shooting.

10

'You know,' Billy said to Luke as he guided the team and wagon along the main street of Crater, Arizona Territory, which had looked so appealing from the crest of the hills but failed to live up to its promise as one drew nearer; it was just another ramshackle desert town where the sun-blistered wooden buildings all seemed to tilt in crazy directions and a few low, solid adobe structures sagged against the earth, 'I don't know if bringing those extra horses along was such a good idea. If Virgil Sly and Boston do reach Crater, they're sure to know who was riding them and want to know what happened to them.'

'We'll sell the horses, and likely be gone on the stage before they ever catch up with us. They had business to take care of in Tucson. Besides, what else was there to do? Leave the horses on the mountain to die?'

'No, no,' Billy said lifting a hand. 'I wouldn't want to do that. I didn't think the roan was going to make it, but he did. We'll stable them both up and they can get all the rest and feed they need. The grays and the wagon, I'll sell them to the first man who offers me a decent price.'

'Then buy stagecoach tickets?'

'For whoever wants to travel on. I know Dee Dee wants to put some more miles between herself and Sly. I'd like to leave as well. I don't want to see those two gunmen again. Susan hasn't said what she plans to do. Have you asked her, Luke?'

'No, I haven't.' Luke turned his head as the wagon rattled its way along the street. 'Hey Tick-Tock, I thought you told us there were a couple of hotels in this town!'

'Well, you just passed one of them,' Tick-Tock, rising to his knees in the bed, told him.

'Where?' Luke said, looking back.

'The place with kind of a green roof.'
Tick-Tock pointed at a weather-beaten
one-story frame building indistinguish-
able from most of the other hastily built
structures in this desert town. Tick-
Tock grinned. 'I never said they were
fancy.'

'Any place with a real bed suits me,'
said Dee Dee, who had had enough of
roughing it.

On the next block of the street, which
seemed to run only for five blocks, they
came upon a two-story white clapboard
building with a shingle reading 'Royal
Crater Hotel,' which seemed a little
pretentious but interested the women.

'That's more like what we had in
mind,' Dee Dee said. 'At least it seems
to be.'

'All right,' said Luke who had spotted
on the opposite side of the street, a
block ahead, a stable with a corral
attached. 'There's what we're looking
for,' he told Billy, pointing that way.
Billy only nodded. Fatigue was obvious
on his face now after the long drive.

'Tick-Tock,' Luke said, 'why don't you go in to the hotel with them and get rooms enough for everyone — two for the women . . .'

'One will suit if it has two beds,' Susan said.

'All right,' Luke answered with some surprise. 'And one for us, if they have one with three beds. Tell them inside that their menfolk with the money will be along shortly. We had to take care of our horses. Got it?'

'I got it,' Tick-Tock said, sliding out of the wagon.

'I'm so stiff from riding in this wagon bed, I don't even know if I can get down,' Dee Dee complained.

'They have beds and a bath,' Luke told her, having read the sign in front of the hotel.

'Out of my way,' Dee Dee commanded, scrambling to her feet. Susan laughed, as did Billy.

'That got her moving,' Billy said.

'She is a lady who likes her comforts,' Luke told him. 'Let's see what we can accomplish at the stable,' he added as Tick-Tock helped Susan to the street. The three men trekked inside.

'What are you thinking of doing?' Billy asked, starting the team again.

'Well, the plan all along was to sell off the team and wagon to get the stage fare. We'll see what we can get for the other two ponies. The roan is pretty beat up. Not of much use or much value at present . . . I was thinking I might keep the buckskin for the time being.'

Billy glanced sideways at Luke as they drew up in front of the stable. There was a scrawny man in a blue-checked shirt, jeans and a straw hat, watching them. 'Why would you want to keep that horse?'

'A man likes to have a horse,' Luke said with a smile.

'I thought . . . look here, Luke are you leaving with Susan on the stage or not?'

'We haven't discussed it,' Luke said, 'and I don't intend to be stranded out here without a horse.'

'Why don't you sit down and talk to her? At least find out what she's thinking?' Billy asked with an edge of frustration in his voice.

'I'd be willing, Billy. But first I have to find out what I'm thinking myself. In the meantime,' he added, 'I'd be happy to have a horse.'

'I never thought it before,' Billy Rafferty said as he looped the reins around the long brake handle and swung down, 'but you are a strange man, Luke Walsh.'

They got a fair price, though the stableman clicked his tongue and frowned over the condition of the red roan. Luke threw in one of the saddles, and that seemed to seal the deal. He did not know whether it was Dan Cummings's or Earl Gross's equipment, but it was made of finely tooled Spanish leather with a silver cap on the pommel, and must have been quite expensive when new: probably purchased when their pockets were filled with gold from some robbery or other shady enterprise.

Luke kept the other saddle, the plainer one, for use on the buckskin, which he had decided to hold on to. He waited outside for Billy to return with the silver money the stableman — who of course had gotten the better of the bargain — had given him.

'Well?' Luke asked.

'Less than I wanted, but more than I expected the way that bird was talking. Enough so that we don't have to worry about meals, hotel rooms or stagecoach tickets.'

Luke rested his hands on Billy's shoulders. 'What do you say we start taking care of those things one at a time. How about we pay for the hotel rooms, then tell Tick-Tock and the girls that we'll be taking them out to dinner after a while?'

'Sounds good to me,' Billy said. They started across the hot, dusty street toward the hotel which, in the fading light of day, looked appealing. More appealing was the thought of a bath and a bed it could provide them.

There was a restaurant connected to the hotel, Luke noted as Billy settled their bill in advance. That would save them the time of searching a strange town for a decent place to eat. Luke could smell steaks frying from the kitchen.

'I think we've reached heaven after all that hell we've been through,' he told Billy as they climbed the staircase to their second floor room. Tick-Tock was already settled in.

'They had to tote up an extra bed, but it looks like we've still got plenty of room, doesn't it?'

'It suits me fine,' Billy said.

'Me, too,' Luke agreed, looking around the small room with its walls papered in white with small blue flowers in the design. The furniture was thin and probably flimsy, but it was the finest place he had seen for a while. A blue curtain fluttered in front of the open window in the warm evening breeze.

'How are the girls set up?' Luke asked, tossing his rifle on to one of the beds and removing his faded, trail-dusty Stetson.

'Their room seems to be real nice,' Tick-Tock said. 'It's all fitted out in red and gold. No one can go over there right now, though — they're having hot water brought up, and a tub to take baths in.'

'Clever of them,' Billy said.

'They are just naturally cleaner animals,' Luke said, sitting on the bed. 'It would have occurred to us sooner or later. Probably later.'

'Look what I picked up at the hotel desk,' Tick-Tock said, tossing a pamphlet on to the bed beside Luke Walsh. 'A stagecoach schedule with the prices to various destinations.'

'That's useful,' Billy said, picking it up. 'Where are you intending to go, Tick-Tock?'

'I'm already there,' Tick-Tock answered with a buck-toothed grin. 'This is where I was headed in the first place, if you'll remember.' Tick-Tock sat on an opposite bed and removed his straw hat. 'I've got a distant relative who lives here — so distant that I don't even know if she's cousin, an aunt or what. Her name's Dusty Donegall — or it *was* Donegall. She's married now.

'She owns a house in town, and her husband's a long-riding man who's sometimes gone for months at a time. Anyway, she said I could stay with her at least until her husband gets back or until I can find a job in Crater, whichever comes first.'

'It's good to have family,' Billy said.

'Most times, I guess,' Luke said in a sort of grumble. No one in his family had ever amounted to much. He rose from the bed. 'I guess we'd better at least rinse off in the basin if we are going to take the women out to supper.'

'I wish I had a decent shirt,' Billy said, looking at his torn, trail-dirty white shirt.

'In a town like this, I'm sure they've seen dirty shirts before,' Luke said.

'After we do some figuring on how much money we need for the stagecoach fare, maybe there'll be enough left over for you to dude yourself up.'

'All I want is a clean shirt,' Billy repeated.

Tick-Tock told him, 'They've got a laundry in this hotel, the women told me. Maybe they can do something with it real quick. The ladies already sent some clothes down there to have them freshened up and ironed.'

'Susan would never have thought of that!' Billy said in amazement.

'Dee Dee would have, first thing,' Luke told him. 'Let's wash up, boys. Anybody got a razor?'

'You can have one sent up,' said Tick-Tock, who seemed to already have gotten the hang of being a hotel dweller.

To the rough-living desert rat, Billy Rafferty, it seemed nothing short of miraculous; to Luke who had coiled up in Dee Dee's hotel room for a while, it was a service he had known about but had forgotten and seldom had the call to use.

Looking slightly more civilized, the three men left their room an hour later and tapped lightly at the ladies' door.

'Who is it?' Dee Dee answered from within.

'Three gentlemen wishing to escort you to your dinner table,' Luke replied.

'Well, for goodness' sake! You gentlemen didn't waste much time cleaning up, did you? You'll just have to wait. One of these ladies is not quite dressed and the other is still soaking in the bathtub.'

'We'll meet you downstairs,' said Luke, who had half-expected such a response.

'What are they doing?' Billy asked as they started toward the staircase. 'I mean — what, that takes so long?'

'Making themselves into the creatures that we are so glad they are.'

'What do we do now?' Billy asked.

'What men always do while they're waiting — we have ourselves a drink.'

'You seem to know a lot about this man-woman thing,' Billy said to Luke as they reached the lobby. Luke looked at him with a frown, then smiled.

'No, I don't. No one does. We just try to keep the truce between us as best we can.'

Dinner in the brightly lit hotel dining room was steak, baked potatoes, corn muffin and apple pie for desert. There was no stopping Tick-Tock, who barely raised his face from his plate until it was cleaned. Billy, on the other hand, glanced at the women with something like amazement now and then.

Dee Dee wore her dark-blue dress, her hair brushed to a glossy shine and pinned up in the style she favored. Susan wore a yellow dress that must have belonged to Dee Dee, and also had her hair pinned up and coiled at the nape of her neck. If Billy watched his cousin with astonishment, Luke looked at her with ill-concealed admiration, his eyes fixed more on her than his food — which was a very good meal, indeed. His plate was still half-full when the others were digging eagerly into their desert pie. Susan caught his eyes on her and returned a pleased smile.

They sat finishing their meal with restaurant coffee, so much better than their boiled rough-country brew, served in small white cups.

'I suppose the stagecoach must run back to Tucson,' Dee Dee said across the table.

'Yes, it does,' said Tick-Tock who had had time to study the schedule. 'Is that where you're going, Miss Dee Dee?'

'I might as well. I don't have much there, but I've got friends and a place I can get a job.'

'The Bluebird?' Luke almost grumbled.

'Why not — I ran out of high ambitions a long time ago, and they treat me right there.'

'How about you, Luke?' Billy asked, 'Is that where you're heading?'

'I don't think so,' Luke answered firmly. Only Dee Dee knew what he meant. It was true that, besides Dee

Dee, no one had actually seen him shoot Marshal Stoddard, but the idea of returning to Tucson seemed too risky. 'I believe I'll stay away from big towns for a while.'

Billy Rafferty said, 'To a desert rat like me, Crater *is* a big town. I might just hang around and see if I can find some kind of work — so long as it doesn't involve a pick and a shovel.'

'There's bound to be something,' Susan put it in.

'You haven't told us what you intend to do, Cousin,' Billy said, finishing off his coffee.

Her blue eyes shifted until they were meeting Luke Walsh's straight on. She answered softly, 'I just haven't made up my mind yet, I guess.'

'Well,' Dee Dee Bright said, 'the stage leaves in the morning, and Virgil Sly and Boston Sears are heading this way. It might be a good time for you to draw up a plan.'

Luke had to let his gaze fall away. Still he had nothing to offer Susan but circling the desert on a stolen horse, trying to elude the law. He couldn't let her live like that. She deserved much better. Men walking past their table cast admiring glances at both women. Susan could easily find a better man, and a better life than any he could offer. In the back of his mind was the idea of riding back to the Havasu Ranch, but now herding cattle seemed a pointless, wearying way to finish his worthless life.

'What about the old woman?' Dee Dee asked. No one caught her reference at first. 'The one staying back on Gun Hill.'

'Emma Sears?' Billy asked.

'That's the one. If Boston is coming to Crater, then she'll be left alone for a long while yet. Maybe Boston Sears doesn't intend to go back to Gun Hill at all. He'd have thought she had enough people around to take care of her.'

'It would serve her right if he doesn't go back,' Susan said bitterly. 'Besides, she's got enough provisions to live on out there for a year.'

'I didn't like her much,' Dee Dee said, 'but I wouldn't wish that on any woman — living alone on a lonely desert mountain. Maybe I could hire someone in Tucson to ride out there and bring her back. You know, it's not her fault her son is a criminal.'

'If you'd be willing to do that, Dee Dee, I think it would be a fine gesture,' Billy said. 'Just so you're not crazy enough to take her under your wing.'

Dee Dee laughed. 'I'll find her a job working in the Bluebird kitchen. If she doesn't like it, she can go her own way.'

That settled, and the waitress eager to clean off their table as the small restaurant began to gather an evening crowd, Dee Dee, Susan and Tick-Tock went upstairs toward their rooms while Billy and Luke went out on to the plankwalk to breathe the night air and have a look at the small town's night denizens. There were more than a few moving about. Some walking, some riding, all moving toward the two facing buildings up the street where lights glared and men's voices and whistles could be heard.

'Want to go have a look at the local saloons?' Luke asked.

'I've never even been in one — living the way I have been,' Billy told him.

'That's why I asked you,' Luke said. 'Myself, I'm not big on places were men see how drunk they can get before they try to start a fight.'

'Kind of pointless, isn't it?' Billy Rafferty said thoughtfully.

'And it can get expensive, making a fool of yourself.'

'Let's forget that idea,' Billy said. He tilted himself against one of the uprights supporting the awning over the hotel's porch and said, 'You know, Luke. With what we know about Virgil Sly and Boston Sears, wouldn't it be a good idea to tell the local law that they're probably making their way toward Crater?'

'I can't see that it is, no,' Luke answered.

'Then we could be sure that Dee Dee and Susan would be protected,' Billy persisted.

'We'll protect them,' Luke said firmly. Billy did not understand Luke's reluctance.

'But if they robbed the Tucson bank, and they are known outlaws, doesn't it make sense to alert the local marshal? It's not like we've done anything wrong, Luke.'

'You've forgotten about Cummings and Gross.'

'That was in self-defense against two other known gunmen!' Billy said, getting excited.

'I'm the one who pulled the trigger,' Luke reminded him. 'I don't want to answer any lawman's questions. Suspicion can fall on anyone. No sense asking for it.'

'I think you're wrong, Luke. We can all testify to the fact that you did nothing wrong.'

Can you testify to the fact that I did not kill Marshal Stoddard back in Tucson? No you can't because I am guilty of it. Luke smiled. 'I say we let the marshal do his own job, and we just get out of town.'

Billy was silent for a minute. Then he said, 'Luke, I have to disagree with you. I generally value your advice, but I have to tell you that I think you're dead wrong this time. We have to keep those murderous thugs away from the girls — and putting them in the marshal's jailhouse is the best way to do that.'

'You do what you conscience dictates,' Luke replied, his eyes searching the streets of the small town, looking for nothing, no one. 'I won't stand in your way.'

'It's the right thing, Luke,' Billy said.

It might have been the right thing for everyone else, but not for Luke Walsh. After discovering Marshal Stoddard's body in Dee Dee's room, any lawman worth his salt would have found out that Dee Dee Bright's 'lover' had quickly left town. Someone working in the hotel would have provided him with Luke's name — he had never kept it a secret. At the least, he figured, there would be fliers out with his name on them as being 'sought for questioning', the phrase they traditionally used on such bills.

Then, whether they managed to get Dee Dee to open up or not, which was highly unlikely, Luke thought, with Sly and Boston in custody any questioning of them would uncover the fact that Luke Walsh had indeed been at the outlaw hideout on Gun Hill. Those two would give up that information happily, pleased to drag Luke down with them, perhaps even to the point of claiming he was a member of their gang.

As to the deaths of Dan Cummings and Earl Gross, why, that could be painted by some clever attorney as a falling-out among thieves if Luke had indeed been a part of that gang. They could claim that Luke felt he had been cut out of the pay-off and wanted the shares that Cummings and Gross were carrying. A jury could be bent to believe all of that if it was fashioned skillfully by a smooth prosecutor.

Standing in the darkness, Luke had the sudden urge to walk to the stable and find out what condition the buckskin horse was in before riding out once again on to the desert and leaving all of this, even Susan, behind. He felt like a man slowly walking the last mile to hell.

Life on Gun Hill hadn't been that terrible after all. Up the street, he saw Billy Rafferty entering the town marshal's office. Luke glanced toward the upper story of the hotel, seeing a light burning in the window of the room that Dee Dee and Susan occupied. He thought he once caught a ripple of feminine laughter from there, but could not be sure above the gathering night-saloon noise.

He re-entered the hotel and climbed the stairs. Tick-Tock was still awake, but obviously sleepy. Luke said nothing as he retrieved his gunbelt and strapped it on. He recovered his Winchester and went out again before a puzzled Tick-Tock could ask a question. Then Luke crossed the street once again and made his way toward the stable opposite as sounds of the night-life continued to echo from uptown and the stars began to gleam against the dome of the cobalt sky.

11

Luke Walsh rode the stubby buckskin horse out on to the desert as the night continued. When the lights of the town had faded from view, no longer casting a pale glow against the sky, he made a rough camp and unsaddled the horse. The horse was a good companion. It offered no recriminations, but accepted the fact that it was time for Luke to ride away from his heavy burdens.

Luke Walsh did not judge himself so lightly. There had been a chance, however slim, that he might have had Susan Rafferty. But what then? Was she to wait for him while he spent years in prison? Possibly it wouldn't have mattered. They probably wouldn't have waited for a trial in Tucson, but have hanged him on the spot. What a proud moment that would have been for her.

No, it was better this way. Let Virgil Sly and Boston Sears get whatever was coming to them. Luke wanted no part of it. He was once again an outlaw on the long desert with no future lying ahead of him. He thought again of returning to the Havasu Ranch, but why take his own trouble to the men there? Some of them, he was sure, would fight for him out of loyalty should a posse come tracking him. The Havasu boys did not deserve to be involved in trouble which was none of their making.

Kicking around to displace any snakes that might lie hidden in the sand, Luke shook out his blanket and settled to the rough ground to watch the lone-some stars and his own life pass before him.

His sleep was a troubled sleep. He engaged himself in arguments all the night long, and at dawn he rose tired and stiff, unsettled and devoid of purpose. He rose to saddle the buckskin, his joints creaking as he moved after his night on the cold desert floor. He was getting too old for this sort of living. His first thoughts were that he might have been too hasty in fleeing, but logic told him that he would have been inviting trouble by remaining in Crater.

What would Susan do now? The question nagged him. Would she travel to Tucson with Dee Dee, who seemed determined to return there? The image of Susan's face, her fine, slender body, was vivid in his mind. He had thrown the saddle over the buckskin's back but had not yet cinched down when he asked the mute, stolid creature:

'What in hell should I do? Remain a coward roaming the desert, or see if there's still a chance I can regain my direction, confidence and possibly even Susan Rafferty?' The animal rolled its eyes, but like all of its kind, had no suggestion to offer. Almost angrily Luke cinched the saddle and swung aboard. He turned the animal's head toward the south, retracing his ride of the night before.

He watched the sun rise to his left, slowly, almost reluctantly entering the skies. The sand began to gleam with morning light. He had to talk to Susan — at least to explain and apologize for running out on her. But before he had reached the outskirts of Crater he heard sounds that reminded him that on this morning the coach for Tucson was pulling out. A bullwhip cracked in the stillness of the morning. Harness creaked as it tightened itself behind the pull of a four-horse team, and the stagecoach rolled out of town heading west. Luke could not make out the passengers through the windows of the distant coach. But he had a burst of fear — or intuition — convincing him that Susan was aboard, and he would never see her lovely face again.

He turned the buckskin to follow after the coach. The road wound through a few scattered scrub oak trees and then faded away on to the flats beyond, stretching out in an arrow-straight line toward Tucson. The four-horse team pulling the coach under the capable hands of a skilled stage driver was rapidly drawing away from him.

He hated to do it, knowing that the little buckskin had already been abused, but he heeled the horse roughly, trying to get its best speed out of it. After a chase of a mile or so, Luke thought that he was gaining ground, but it was little enough. The stubby little buckskin was wearying, and it could not have ever been very fast.

Still he urged it on, riding bent over the withers, his hat brim flapping back in the wind. The road bent slightly to avoid a low knoll and Luke decided to cut the trail there to try gaining ground. Mentally apologizing to the struggling animal, he rode it roughly on, crested the knoll, looked ahead . . .

He saw the hold-up men halting the stage.

They were too far off to identify, but Luke was familiar with the black horse that Virgil Sly rode. The animal one of the robbers was mounted on was very similar, indeed. The other man was a bulky rider, as big as Boston Sears. Both wore bandannas over their faces. He could not be certain, but if it wasn't Sears and Sly, there were a lot of strange circumstances at play here.

He urged the buckskin down the slope as the highwaymen prompted the passengers to step down by waving their pistols in their direction. The stage-coach driver was already out of his box, standing near his team with his hands hoisted.

As Luke rode swiftly, carefully forward, he caught a glimpse of the passengers as they emerged from the coach. A woman in blue satin stepped daintily to the ground, hands raised. Then a slender young man in jeans and a white shirt. Lastly a blonde wearing yellow. It was Susan — he would know her from a mile away! Dee Dee, Billy and Susan, headed for Tucson together. As Luke approached the scene he unlimbered his Winchester. The hold-up men still had all of their attention fixed on the passengers. Now and then one or the other would glance back down the road, but neither looked in his direction.

The clopping of the buckskin's hoofs were too loud in Luke's ears as he rode it across a stretch of hardpan, steel shoes clacking over red stone, and the sounds brought the head of the man he took to be Boston Sears around. A shout went up. A bullet was loosed in his direction. At the first report of the gun, Luke saw Billy Rafferty grab his cousin's hand and roll under the coach with her. Dee Dee Bright stood as if dazed in the middle of the confusion.

Luke had opened up with his Winchester while the pony he rode was still on the run, and his shots missed widely. He felt the buckskin stumble and lurch, then the horse was out from under him. Struck by a bullet, or simply played out, he could not tell. Luke kicked free of the stirrups and rolled aside, knocking his shoulder painfully as the horse went down.

Both of the men below were firing their pistols in his direction. They carried no rifles, none being expected to be needed for this little job, and their marksmanship with handguns at this distance was not up to the task.

Luke was up on one knee now, taking careful aim with his Winchester. He deliberately adjusted his aim for drop and fired at Boston Sears's great grizzly chest. The man's hands went up, flailing wildly as his body was slammed against the coach. Shifting his sights to Virgil Sly, Luke triggered off another round. He could almost see the panic in the badman's eyes as he fired back wildly with his Colt revolver. Luke heard a woman scream as he squeezed off another rifle shot — in fear or pain, he could not tell.

The .44-.40 slug from Luke's Winchester spun Virgil Sly around like a faltering top. He took two steps forward, fired his pistol again and then fell face forward against the desert sands where he lay still beside Boston Sears.

Luke returned to the fallen buckskin horse which, astoundingly, had come to its feet again, apparently unharmed. He swung into the saddle and rode it at a walk it down the slope toward where the coach stood. The driver and his passengers watched his approach.

As Luke swung down from the exhausted buckskin, Billy Rafferty approached him to shake his hand, a wide grin on his face. 'By God, Luke, you do pick the times to show up!' Billy said in greeting.

Susan was still rising from beneath the coach where they had hidden to get out of the path of the flying bullets. She looked stunned, angry and beautiful. Dee Dee Bright was leaning against the stagecoach, holding her hand against her stomach. Dee Dee's face was drained of color. When she moved her hand away from her abdomen, it came away red.

The stagecoach driver had now joined them, and he looked back down the road leading to Crater, where a storm of dust could be seen nearing them.

'Too late as usual,' the leathery old stage driver said with some rancor. 'Unless I miss my guess, that's Marshal Suggs and a posse coming.'

The stage driver was right. In a few minutes a dozen men riding foam-flecked ponies drew up, surrounding the coach, a fine scattering of dust drifting behind them. Suggs swung down from his palomino. His badge, worn on a black leather vest, glinted in the harsh sunlight. He wore a huge sombrero and a wildly flourishing red mustache, perhaps to compensate for his relatively small body. He might not have been imposing in stature, but nevertheless he had the hard, no-nonsense eyes of a long-time officer of the law.

'You're a little late, Ray,' the stage driver said, stepping forward. 'As usual,' he muttered under his breath.

'Someone reported shots being fired. It does take a little time to gather a posse,' Suggs said defensively. 'What's the story here?'

'The story,' Susan Rafferty said, 'is that we have a badly injured woman here who has to get to a doctor!'

Suggs looked at the gunshot Dee Dee, glanced at the driver and said, 'Better turn around, Earl — we have to take her back to Crater.'

'I can't miss my schedule!' the driver complained.

'You have to, if I tell you so,' Suggs said firmly. Susan and Billy were picking Dee Dee up from the ground and trying to place her gently in the coach. Suggs looked directly at Luke and demanded, 'Now what's going on here?'

'That's Virgil Sly,' Luke said, studying the dead man, 'and that's Boston Sears. They were both Red Butte riders.

They held up a bank in Tucson yesterday. You'd better check their saddle-bags for evidence.'

'You seem to know a lot about matters,' Suggs commented.

'I guess I do,' Luke had to admit.

Suggs frowned and said to one of his men who was standing near by with a shotgun in his hands, 'Better check out their saddle-bags, Nate.' The man nodded and turned away.

The driver was backing and filling, trying to turn the coach without getting bogged down in the sand beside the road. Suggs said, 'I guess I'd better ride inside with the rest of you. Someone needs to tell me what this is all about.'

'I told you last night,' Billy Rafferty said, overhearing.

'You can tell me again,' Suggs said implacably. 'I like a good story.'

'Ray!' the man who had been sent to check the outlaws' saddle-bags called out. 'There's near five thousand dollars in their pouches. Most of it still has a Tucson National band around it.'

'Leave it where it is, and tow those ponies of theirs on behind.'

'You want me to ride along?' Luke asked. 'I can't leave my own horse.'

'No,' Suggs said after a minute's heavy thought. 'You ride inside with the rest of us.' Then: 'Nate! Put a loop around the buckskin's neck and bring it along as well.'

The posse member nodded his head and uncoiled his lasso as Marshal Suggs gestured for Luke Walsh to clamber aboard the stage, which was now turned toward Crater once more. Inside, the three men settled in uncomfortably while on the opposite bench Susan tried to tend to Dee Dee, who was obviously badly wounded. Susan stroked the woman's hair and forehead, patting her face with a handkerchief damp with canteen water. The driver's whip cracked over the ears of the four-horse team and they started forward, with a lurch, the stagecoach rocking.

'Now,' Ray Suggs said as they began

rolling smoothly across the desert, flanked by the posse, 'tell me everything that happened.'

'I told you most of it last night,' Billy said as they rocked along.

'Maybe I should have listened better,' Suggs said. He seemed slightly angry at himself.

'Today, as soon as we hit open ground, Boston Sears and Sly held up the stage.'

'Wanting what? More money? They seem to have already had plenty.'

'Sly wanted Dee Dee back,' Luke put in, gesturing toward the injured girl. 'She was his woman. He wasn't going to let her get away.'

The marshal looked to where Dee Dee lay, her head on Susan's lap. 'I see — all for love,' he replied, scoffing lightly at the tale.

'There's more to it,' Luke said, but got no further. They all watched as Dee Dee lifted a hand and tried to sit up. She had obviously been listening. She never made it to a sitting position, but her eyes were wide open and clear. She fixed them on Suggs.

'Sly was after me,' Dee Dee said in a faint voice, 'Because I saw him kill Marshal Will Stoddard in Tucson. There was bad blood between them.'

'Are you sure?' Suggs said, stiffening.

'It happened in my room! I was there. That's why I fled Tucson,' Dee Dee said, her voice growing fainter yet. 'You think I wanted to stay around and testify against Virgil Sly?' She lifted her head a bare inch and directed a wink at Luke Walsh, then it fell back again.

'I'll be damned,' Suggs said, apparently happy to have been able to solve the murder of the Tucson marshal. His mood shifted. He slapped his thigh and turned to Luke Walsh. 'How did you just happen to come along today?' he asked.

'I was out late last night,' Luke improvised. 'When my woman caught the stage, I had missed it and I knew she was bound to be pretty angry. I was trying to catch up with her,' he finished with a shrug.

'And you got Sly and Boston Sears?' Suggs asked with narrowed eyes.

'He did,' Billy spoke up. 'Here these bandits were, brandishing guns around me and my cousin. Luke knew who they were. What else would any good citizen do?'

'I'm not questioning that,' Suggs replied. 'I was just thinking how much reward might come due to Walsh for taking down the bank robbers, recovering the money they had stolen and taking down the murderer of Marshal Stoddard. It will be quite a bit, I'll tell you.'

'We could use it,' Luke said, reaching over to take Susan's pale hand. 'But it looks like I've already gotten my reward.'

★   ★   ★

They gathered at the chapel in Crater. Susan looked incredibly beautiful in white. She wore a single yellow flower in her hair. Dee Dee had insisted that she must attend, despite the fact that she was still supposed to remain in bed. Billy wheeled her to the church in a wicker wheelchair, wearing a new brown suit that he had purchased with the returned fare from the stage line tickets.

Tick-Tock also managed to attend along with his distant relative, Dusty Donegall, who was much younger and prettier than Luke had expected. Dusty was dolled up prettily in a light blue dress and little blue hat tilted on her head.

Marshal Suggs had also managed to show up. He and Luke had not exactly become friends, but they were familiar acquaintances, and Ray Suggs had to respect Luke after the role he had played in breaking up the Red Butte gang. And Luke Walsh was a solid citizen now, having been rewarded by the territory and the bank as well as the stage line for his efforts.

It wasn't a lot of money, but it was

enough for a man to get married on.

After the brief ceremony they met in a small hall the church reserved for such occasions and toasted to everyone's fortune and luck.

'What do you say, Billy?' Luke said as they found themselves alone in the small gathering. 'What's your new plan? Going on to Tucson, still?'

'Maybe,' Billy Rafferty said, shaking his head. He sipped from his wine glass. 'The first thing I'm going to do is make sure that Dee Dee recovers. I've been to see her every day, you know. The more I get to know her, the more I've decided that she is quite a remarkable woman.'

'She is that,' Luke was forced to agree. The light in Billy's eyes was not from the wine he was drinking. He was looking at the dark-haired woman sitting in a wheelchair in the corner.

'I'd better talk to her for a minute before Susan and I leave,' Luke said. He strode across the wooden floor of the hall and took Dee Dee's hand. She smiled up at him.

'Happy?' she asked.

'You bet I am,' he answered, looking across the room to where Susan stood, searching the gathered group for him. Their eyes met and Susan gestured, with a slight sloping of her head, that she was ready to leave.

'I've got to go, Dee Dee. Get well.'

'I will, Luke.' Her voice lowered, and still holding his hand, she asked. 'Are we even now?'

Luke laughed, and he said. 'Darlin', now *I* owe *you*!'

It was a warm, clear day outside the church and as Luke stepped out with Susan on his arm, people surging after them, Luke paused for a moment and considered: Crater wasn't such a bad little town after all.

Susan went to tiptoes and kissed him, and they started on their way home, the laughter and sounds of enjoyment from the folks behind them following them to the buggy which stood waiting to carry them forward into a new life, a million miles away from Gun Hill.

We do hope that you have enjoyed reading this large print book.

Did you know that all of our titles are available for purchase?

We publish a wide range of high quality large print books including:
Romances, Mysteries, Classics
General Fiction
Non Fiction and Westerns

Special interest titles available in large print are:
The Little Oxford Dictionary
Music Book, Song Book
Hymn Book, Service Book

Also available from us courtesy of Oxford University Press:
Young Readers' Dictionary
(large print edition)
Young Readers' Thesaurus
(large print edition)

For further information or a free brochure, please contact us at:
Ulverscroft Large Print Books Ltd.,
The Green, Bradgate Road, Anstey,
Leicester, LE7 7FU, England.
Tel: (00 44) 0116 236 4325
Fax: (00 44) 0116 234 0205

The members of the wagon train called him 'Mr Gunn'. A good name, and he'd earned it — but it wasn't his . . . That was the trouble: he didn't know *who* he was since he'd woken in a Union Army camp, wounded and wearing a dead man's tunic. Seeking out the widow of Captain Landis, the uniform's owner, Gunn finds no answers — only further questions. But when he is hounded as a Johnny Reb and falsely accused of murder, it's left to Beth Landis to mount a rescue mission . . .

SOUTH TO SONORA

Michael Stewart

After a ten-year prison term for killing a man he'd found molesting a girl, all Tom Jericho wants is a quiet life. But, the day before his release, the warden offers him a deal: if Tom infiltrates the notorious Crane gang and uncovers details of their plans, he'll be set up with enough money to buy a patch of land to farm. All he has to do is get himself arrested for murder — then spring his old friend Lee Crane from the prison train . . .

TOM RIDER'S RECKONING

Rob Hill

In prosperous El Cobarde, the respected sheriff Tom Rider is happily anticipating his retirement. But, barely hours after Tom hands over the reins of command, notorious local lawbreaker Jeb Deeds escapes from his prison train and storms the streets with dynamite, pursuing a vendetta against the eminent town founders. For a long-buried secret is about to emerge, and Deeds intends to bring a bloody reckoning to this town built on foundations of murder and treachery . . .

NIGHT OF THE GUNSLINGER

I. J. Parnham

With the town marshal laid up with a broken leg, Deputy Rick Cody must stand alone to protect New Town during a night of mayhem. At sunup Edison Dent will stand trial for Ogden Reed's murder — but Rick doubts his guilt. With only one night to uncover the truth, his task is made harder when the outlaw Hedley Beecher plots to free the prisoner. Meanwhile, Ogden's brother Logan vows to kill Edison and anyone who stands in his way . . .